SEEKING
SARA

Maurine Gillberry

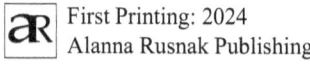 First Printing: 2024
Alanna Rusnak Publishing

Library and Archives Canada Cataloguing in Publication
CIP data on file with the National Library and Archives

ISBN trade paperback edition: 978-1-990336-86-7

Alanna Rusnak Publishing is an imprint of Chicken House Press

282906 Normanby/Bentinck Townline
Durham, Ontario, Canada, N0G 1R0
www.chickenhousepress.ca

In Memory of

my Parents
Les and Jean Pitt (nee Wilson)

and

my Grandmother
Ada Osborne (nee Pitt)

Your stories are my stories.

SEEKING SARA

Maurine Gillberry

Chapter One

Rural Ontario | 2005

My *heart pounded in my ears and I* *struggled to breathe. Total blackness surrounded me. I couldn't move and couldn't fill my lungs. This was what it felt like to suffocate. I was in a coffin! How was that possible?*

A low steady roar enveloped me, adding to my paralyzing panic. The relentless noise had to be a train. I was in a coffin on a train, with no memory of how this had happened.

Piercing flashes of light exploded all around me, and I realized with horror that the train was on fire. Then a tremendous noise slammed into me. The train had crashed! Was I going to die inside a coffin?

Somehow, the crash shook me loose and the coffin fell completely away...

I opened my eyes to a searing streak of light, and briefly glimpsed tiny blue flowers on wallpaper before darkness engulfed me again. With considerable effort, I pulled down my hunched shoulders, stretched out my stiff legs, and took a deep breath. Then there was more noise—a familiar tune repeating itself over and over. Slowly, I turned my head towards the sound and picked up my cell phone on the bedside table. "Hello?"

"Sara girl," my grandmother said. "Get out of that attic and come downstairs with us until the storm is over."

The sound of her voice instantly grounded me. My breathing calmed, my heart rate slowed, my mind cleared. It felt like I had just kaleidoscoped down the funnel of a tornado and been spit out onto my bed, deposited back into my real life. Everything made sense again. I was in my room at the farm, a raging thunderstorm shattered the night outside. Through the skylight, another ball of lightening shot across my vision, and was immediately followed by a crack of thunder that made the old house shudder. I reached to turn on the lamp, but of course there was no power. Sitting up too quickly caused a wave of dizziness, so I paused and took a couple deep breaths, then clicked on my cell phone for light, grabbed my sweatshirt from the end of the bed, and headed down two flights of stairs.

My grandparents were at the table in the small sitting room. In front of them, three tapered candles glowed, and two teapots cuddled in pink and brown crocheted cozies.

"The water started boiling just as the power went out," explained Grandma. "Come, I've poured you half a cup. The pink teapot is just hot water so you can make it as weak as you want, and your Grandpa brought the honey for you."

Gratefully, I sat down, poured extra water into my cup, and dolloped in some honey. Wrapping both hands around the mug, I brought the sweet warmth up to my face and breathed it in.

"Girl, your hands are shaking," said Grandma, and placed one of her papery smooth hands over mine. "Are you alright?"

Taking a big shaky breath, I told them about the nightmare—the first time the little girl theme and the coffin theme were tangled together (like a two-for-one special) with the storm adding some fresh layers of terror.

"You know I sometimes have this dream about a weird little girl, right?" Two white-topped heads nodded. "Well, she was in the initial part of this one. I was on a train and had just ordered lunch when I realized the dining car was suddenly completely deserted. All the people had vanished. And the noise of the train became really, really loud, which I guess was the thunder. I was already starting to panic, when that eerie little girl suddenly materialized right in front of me."

"Nightmares don't hold too much to logic," Grandma noted. "But what do you mean by eerie? What was she like?"

"Well, for one thing, she was translucent. I could kind of see through her. And she just stared at me without blinking, like she was wanting something from me, or maybe accusing me of something. She was quite grubby looking, barefoot. She wore an old fashioned dress, and had long, straggly, reddish hair."

"Oh boy, another redhead," Grandpa piped up. "That *is* scary."

Grandma and I—the first and second redheads to whom he was referring—laughed and I could feel the tension easing out of me.

"And then the little waif whispered my name. Like in every dream of her, she said, 'Sara,' three times… in such a plaintive, pleading little voice. And she stared at me… or through me, with big, luminous eyes."

"That is so unsettling that she says your name," mused Grandma, and rubbed my back a bit. "Then what happened?"

"Well, the roaring of the train got louder and louder, and my panic spiralled. But then suddenly, in the dream it was completely dark. I couldn't see anything at all, and along with the blackness came constriction. My arms, my legs, my head were suddenly cramped as though something was pushing in on me from all sides."

I didn't tell my grandparents that the constriction in the nightmare seemed to be a coffin. It didn't seem right to speak of coffin nightmares to octogenarians. My grandparents shook their heads as I continued. "Then there were piercing explosions of light and I was certain the train was on fire. That would have been the lightning, so maybe I was half-awake by then. When another really big boom came, I thought the train had crashed, and well, it seemed like that would be the end of me."

"Oh Sara," Grandma said. "I'm so sorry. How dreadful. I feel so badly you were way up there all by yourself."

"Grandma, you know I love that attic room, but it is pretty dramatic in a big storm."

Then Grandpa added, "I remember that really big crack of thunder just before your Grandma called you. It was a real close one."

"So yes, that big crash seemed to kind of shake me loose a bit. I was actually all scrunched up in a tight ball, but then I started to slowly move my arms and legs. I was quite stiff, like I'd been that way for awhile, but it couldn't have been very long. Finally, I opened my eyes right when a searing streak of lightning shot over the skylight. That's when I saw the tiny blue flowers on the wallpaper, and started to realize that I was not, in fact, on a train... crashed or otherwise. And then you phoned, Grandma, and as soon as I heard your voice, my head cleared. I immediately knew where I was and what was happening."

My grandparents shook their heads and patted each of my hands. Then Grandma topped up my tea while Grandpa nudged the honeypot closer to me.

At that moment, a particularly sharp crash of thunder made us all jump, and we turned our attention to the nearby window. The furious storm alternated between sideways sheeting rain and hail the size of peas that bounced off the windows and briefly carpeted the ground. The wind howled and we cringed at the crack of tree branches breaking somewhere beyond the front of the house.

"I hope that's not the old maple," Grandma lamented.

We stayed up for almost two hours, listening to the storm and sometimes chatting about family and upcoming events.

At one point, Grandpa asked, "What happened to that nice fella we met at Christmas time at your place? Are you still seeing him?"

"No, I'm not. He was great the first few weeks we were together, but then he became a jealous, moody guy. He was always nicer when we were around other people, but when it was just the two of us, he could be quite mean and nasty. I had to kick him to the curb, Grandpa."

"Is that so?" he said, shaking his head.

"Well, good for you, dear," Grandma piped in. "You shouldn't take that kind of behaviour from anyone. You deserve better."

"But Grandma, I just don't know if there are any nice guys left. They often seem nice in the beginning but then they turn into jerks."

She patted my shoulder. "Oh, the right fellow will come along, dear, maybe when you least expect it. You'll find each other."

Eventually, the rain relented into a more downward direction; the thunder grumbled off into the distance, and all that was left of the lightening were small protests along the western horizon. My grandparents slowly rose from their chairs, and with Grandpa shining a flashlight for her, Grandma pulled around her walker. Just before heading off to their main floor bedroom, she suggested I sleep on the sitting-room couch.

"Great idea, Grandma." After blowing out the candles, I plopped down on the couch and pulled over a nearby blanket.

I had been staying with my grandparents for a week and a half, ever since finishing my final semester at university and thus completing my Teacher Education Degree. After five years of university, I felt drained, and Mom had suggested I spend the summer at the farm. She said I needed some down time, but I figured she just didn't want me staying alone in our Toronto house. Mom was a university professor in the area of Environment and Development, and since January had been on a one-year exchange to the London School of Economics, a job and location that was her dream come true. Dad was a semi-retired optometrist, who had been in London with her for the last month, and would stay until the beginning of August, when he would return to cover staff holidays at his clinic. I had struggled with nightmares, anxiety, and panic attacks over the last year, but the nightmares had never bothered me at the farm before, and I was disappointed they had now invaded my safe house.

After a couple hours of sleeping restlessly on the couch, I was startled awake by blinding light. When my senses caught up, I realized the power had returned, and since the lamps had not been turned off, they filled the space with sudden light. The rain had stopped and the world seemed calm. As I settled my racing heart, I looked around the room, which had not changed since I was a little girl. Same gold and orange flowered couch. Same small round table and chair set. Same pictures of birds and a fall woods scene on the walls. Same knick-knacks displayed on the wide window sills, with the same crocheted lace doilies beneath each one. I took comfort in this sameness, this solidness, this past. Smiling to myself, I got up and turned off the lights.

On Wednesday morning, I slept in until ten o'clock. When I ambled out from the sitting room, the house seemed empty, so I threw on a jacket, wandered out the back door and found the old folks surveying the storm damage. Grandpa walked with his outside cane, which was an old shovel handle, and wore rubber boots, his barn jacket, and an old brown corduroy cap. Grandma trundled along in her motorized scooter, and was well-bundled in a winter coat, toque, and mitts.

Smiling fondly, I walked up to them. They had been married for sixty-two years, had lived on this farm for fifty-eight years, and I cherished the privilege of being their granddaughter.

"Well, here's our sleeping beauty," Grandpa said, putting his hand on my shoulder.

"How are you feeling this morning?" Grandma asked.

While assuring them I was fine, I noticed the big maple tree along the lane that was almost split in half.

"Whoa, Grandpa," I said, pointing to the damage. "I think we're going to need some help with that one!"

He nodded in agreement. "Scott will come down with the chainsaw. I'll give him a call when I get inside."

Scott was married to my cousin Stacy and they lived with their two young kids on a dairy farm a few kilometres north on the County Line. Scott grew up on that farm and about three years ago took it over from his father. He also rented land on my grandparent's farm and was quite diligent about helping out Grandma and Grandpa as needed.

The three of us stood on the knoll between the lane

and the pond lawn, with the house behind us, and surveyed the property. It was a chilly morning and I pulled up the hood of my jacket and crammed my hands deep into the pockets. Spring had been very late in her take-over this year, with winter clinging by his fingernails, staying on like an unwanted house guest who didn't know enough to leave. The blizzards and freezing rain still raged in the middle of April while I was hunkered down studying for my last exam. High winds and heavy layers of ice had caused significant damage to the trees, leaving many of them as sad, deformed remnants of their former selves. They remained in their grey winter garb with no hint of spring colour, seeming to lack the energy to move forward into spring. The entire landscape looked exhausted and spent.

Except for the willows. I loved the willows. Undaunted and optimistic, they forged ahead of the rest. They already sported a beginning hue of green, like a very pale wash of watercolour. And in the fall, the willows were always the last to surrender their leaves, stubbornly clinging to them long after their neighbours had abandoned the effort. Grandpa always complained about the messiness of the willows, but I just loved their draping grace and their exuberant, outgoing personalities.

Grandpa and I spent part of the day tackling the debris on the lawns. Scott was coming the next morning with the chainsaw to deal with the devastated old maple. In the afternoon, Grandma and Grandpa departed to a friend's place for dinner and an inevitable evening of cards. I headed to the second floor bathroom to get cleaned up.

At the end of my shower, I was inside the stall, wringing out my long mane of hair, when through the fog of the glass door, I saw her. Gasping, I froze in place and stared at the little ghost.

She looked exactly the same as in my dreams—a bedraggled little girl with holes in her oversized clothes, who stared at me with a disturbing, unblinking intensity. Then in a plaintive but ominous voice, she spoke my name, "Sara," and looked at me with urgent expectancy, as if she had asked a question and desperately needed an answer. Knowing what would happen next, a lump rose in my throat that I could not swallow away. Then sure enough, she repeated my name two more times.

Feeling like I'd been kicked in the stomach and couldn't catch my breath, I was surprised when my trembling right hand reached out and placed itself flat against the damp door, fingers spread wide. In unnerving slow motion, the child raised her hand and moved it towards my own, but en route, it transformed from a five finger stretch into a one finger point aimed straight at my chest. A ragged pain stabbed through my heart, and then she was gone.

Shakily, I opened the shower door and glanced around the now empty room. Wrapping myself in a towel, with another around my hair, I sat down unsteadily on the edge of the bathtub. It felt like my lungs had collapsed, and although I tried to concentrate on my breathing, my mind immediately ricocheted to Uncle Ray.

My Uncle Ray had been diagnosed with schizophrenia when I was a kid, and his symptoms included hallucinations. Was I beginning down that same sinister passageway? I vigorously shook my head and managed a big breath. No! It was probably from the stress of university, not getting enough sleep, and not knowing what I should do with the rest of my life. Either that or I was actually going crazy. Time would tell, I supposed.

After a few more deep breaths, I went up to my bedroom, put on pajamas, then headed downstairs and turned on the TV. After flicking channels, I found an acceptable movie that was about to start, and went into the kitchen to rummage in the fridge for left-overs. There was a reasonable selection, so I zapped a plateful in the microwave and returned to the movie. At ten o'clock, my grandparents arrived home and went off to bed. Reluctantly, I decided to do the same. I read until midnight and then some time later, finally fell asleep.

But sure enough, in the early morning hours, the Raving Rasputin nightmare rounded off the stellar line-up of weirdness. Rasputin (so named because he reminded me of the crazed lover of the Russian Tsarina) had long, dirty-grey hair, gaps in his mouth between brown teeth, and white bulging eyes with intense black pupils. As always, he was stretched out on a cot with his arms restrained in what I think was a straight jacket, plus he was tied to the bed by a strap around his waist. He was as mad as he could be, in both senses of the word, and incessantly spewed out Bible quotes and spittle, while straining his upper body from side to side.

Upon waking, I found myself desperately thrashing back and forth, apparently mimicking Rasputin's crazed movements. In an effort to clear away the image of the demented old man, I sat up, gulped in big breaths, and forcefully waved my arms above my head.

Blast you, Rasputin, I do not want you at the farm! I didn't want any of them at the farm!

Then an unwanted thought chilled me to the marrow and froze my movements. What if Rasputin appeared in the daytime like the little girl? My heart rate soared, sudden goose bumps shivered down my arms, and the bottom dropped out of my stomach.

Chapter Two

I never did get back to sleep, and was glad when morning finally arrived. Before long, Scott also arrived and we tackled the old maple. Scott was about ten years older than I, solidly built, and a little taller than Grandpa. While he roared about with the chainsaw, Grandpa and I loaded tree branches onto the farm wagon and hauled them away. Being busy helped keep my mind off the nightmares and the disturbing little ghost, and by late morning the job was complete. Good timing, as the wind started whipping the tree branches around and the sky darkened. During lunch it began to pour, and I envisioned a nerve-racking afternoon stretching out before me.

Sipping my obligatory cup of tea at the end of the meal, I asked, "Is there anything I could do in the house this afternoon to help out?"

"Well," said Grandpa, "I could surely use some assistance cleaning out the little back cellar. How would you feel about that?"

"Let's do it!" I exclaimed, thinking this would be a job to keep my mind off crazies and spooks.

The cellar smelled musty and dampish and over the next couple of hours, I hauled a wide range of useless stuff to the adjoining garage for later transport to the dump. Besides junk, we uncovered some interesting things in the cellar. There was a puzzling heavy iron gadget about the size of a kettle, which had a stand at one end, and two thick prong-type things at the other.

Grandpa refused to explain it to me, but teased me with fake hints, which resulted in some pretty wild guesses on my part.

The milkiness that softened his blue eyes did not hide the twinkle, and finally, with a smirk on his face, he said, "It has to do with footwear."

"It's a shoe-form!" I exclaimed. "You would put a shoe over it to hammer on the sole and stuff." Nailed it!

"It's called a shoe anvil, and my mother brought it from England with her when she came over on a ship in the 20s," explained Grandpa.

It belonged to my Great Grandmother! How cool. Eventually we also unearthed a weird little hammer—more like a tiny iron post—that went with it. By late afternoon, with the cellar in pretty good shape, we surfaced to the main floor and were surprised to see the rain had stopped and the sun was back out. Grandma suggested we all go out for some fresh air and check over the grounds.

So with Grandma in her scooter and Grandpa with his trusty shovel handle, we wandered down towards the pond and examined the birch tree, the reigning queen of the farm lawns, who had weathered the winter remarkably unscathed.

Looking out across the pond, I felt so much love for this farm. It was great to see water, as opposed to the ice that still covered the pond on the day of my arrival, less than two weeks previously. The great blue heron that had stood dubiously on the frozen surface that day would surely be very pleased with this transformation as well.

My grandparents decided to inspect around the perimeter of the pond, which seemed a long way for Grandpa to manage on the rough ground, so I inconspicuously stayed close in case he tripped. We crossed the little bridge over the spillway, with the rush of water tumbling beneath it, hurrying to reach the ditch and charge north to parts unknown.

"How big is the pond?" I asked.

"It's about an acre," Grandpa replied. "Around the same size as an NFL football field."

"But rounder," I added. Then my mind wandered back to the unearthed shoe anvil. "How old was Great Grandma when she came to Canada?" I asked, "And what was her name?"

"Her name was Sadie," Grandpa said, "and it was just after the First World War, so I think she was around 25."

"My age," I said in surprise. "I guess back then if you immigrated to Canada from England, you wouldn't really expect to see your family or friends ever again would you?"

"No, not really, although one of her sisters did immigrate too, a few years later," Grandpa responded.

Then Grandma added, "Gran came over on a ship completely by herself and she was stone-deaf, having lost her hearing while working in a boot factory in London. The ship disembarked in Montreal. She probably didn't even realize the people there spoke French! She could lip-read quite well, but not in French. Hard to imagine all she went through."

"Wow," I said. "That's amazing. But Grandma, let me get this straight... you called Grandpa's mother Gran?"

Grandma smiled. "Everyone called your Grandfather's mother either Granny or Gran... even people who weren't related to her."

Laughing, I said, "Cool. I like it. Okay, so she was coming across the ocean, alone and deaf, and ended up in Montreal. What did she do?"

"Well, she somehow managed to get a job in a shoe factory there, probably taking that anvil and hammer with her to show she knew how to use them."

We were at the far end of the pond by then and Grandma stopped to study a greening daffodil patch which promised an upcoming sunny display. Moving on, we came to the lone willow, and I threw a couple fallen branches onto the edge of the adjoining field so Grandma could drive through.

Grandma continued her story. "In a corner of the shoe factory in Montreal, there was what Gran called a "modern" machine that no one knew how to use, and with the language problem she couldn't make anyone understand she had operated the same machine in England." Grandma laughed and shook her head. "Oh, she was still spitting mad about that when she told me decades later!"

Great Grandma must have been a tough lady. We meandered over the second bridge, stopping briefly to watch the water dash towards the pond, then continued into the willow garden. In another month, the three elderly willows would form a living, swaying cathedral in this space.

We had successfully circumnavigated the pond without Grandpa stumbling or Grandma rolling into the water, and as we headed towards the farmhouse, I asked them how old it was. Simultaneously, they stopped moving forward and searched each other's faces for memory support.

Grandma mused out loud, "Well, Uncle Bob said he remembered this house being built, but he was quite young… maybe 4 or 5. Uncle Bob was 85 when he died, but how long ago did he die?"

After much conferring back and forth, they eventually decided the house was built around 1898.

"So it's over a hundred years old," I added. "Wow."

We all gazed at the house, a no-nonsense cement block affair, but its serious demeanour was lightened considerably by the lime green window and door trim that Grandma had chosen a few years earlier. Most of the family cringed at this colour decision, but I loved it. It was just so Grandma. Her favourite colours were green, orange, and purple, so considering these other possibilities, lime green didn't seem too bad. Facing the pond, the house sported a small screened-in porch and a larger deck. My grandparents explained that in the early eighties, they had added the two-car garage, with family room and bedroom over top, but on the same level as the main house.

"We converted the attic into a bedroom at the same time," Grandma added. "We really didn't need it, but I just always thought it would make such a great bedroom."

I loved that bedroom so was in total agreement. Gazing up at the window in the peak facing us, I could see the curtains blowing a bit in the breeze.

Then I thought, *no wait, that window doesn't have curtains, it just has a blind that I always leave up.* A tingle raced up my spine and my heart started hammering. *It was the little ghost... it was her dress blowing! Oh my god, she was in my room looking down at me!* My legs went weak and the air seemed too thin for me to catch my breath. Squinting sideways at my grandparents, I noted they appeared completely unperturbed.

I cleared my throat, swallowed, cleared my throat again, and finally managed to blurt out, "Was that attic window always there, or did you put it in?"

They both gazed up at the window. "Oh, we put that one in, and the skylight of course," Grandma said. "The window in the peak on other side was always there."

As they looked upwards, I scrutinized their faces for an indication that they saw anything weird, but nope, they definitely only saw a window.

Grandma noticed me studying them. "What?" she asked.

My mind scrambled for something intelligent to say. "Oh, I was just thinking about how long you've lived here and the changes you've made."

"Been here since March of '47," Grandpa stated. "Record snowfall for Grey County that winter, and our new neighbours met us several blocks east with horses and cutters 'cause the cars couldn't get any further. Some of the drifts were so high, I could reach out and touch the telephone wires."

"Eugene," Grandma added. "Remember in April, there was still so much snow that you and a gang of men hand-shovelled a path ahead of the snow ploughs on some of the roads. Other men did the same for the trains as well."

Having trouble concentrating, I thought I had missed something. "Wait, what do you mean?"

"They had to lower the drifts by hand to a level the machines could handle," she explained.

"Wow, that is a lot of snow," I managed to say, then added, "Hey, I think I'll keep walking... go on back the lane a bit."

Taking a few shaky steps away from the house, I forced myself to look back up at the window. She was gone. Had I really seen her? Yes, I knew I had. But was she a hallucination? Was I actually developing schizophrenia, or was there such a thing as a real ghost?

Chapter Three

That evening, I contemplated sleeping in one of the second floor bedrooms, but eventually refused to give in to my fear and slept in my own room. After reading in bed for a couple hours, I drifted to sleep and was surprised to wake up to bright sunshine streaming through the windows, having had no visitors of any kind during the night.

Grandpa and I spent part of the morning cleaning up the willow garden. By ten o'clock, when we had the tractor bucket pretty much filled with twigs and last year's leaves, Scott drove in the lane. He waved but kept going around the barn and beyond. Returning a short time later, he stopped, climbed out of the truck, and headed towards us with the Grey County farmer stride: shoulders and arms back, long purposeful steps. "Hey, how are you two doing today?"

Grandpa leaned on a rake, and with a twinkle in his eye, deadpanned a favourite line: "Well, I'm being good, but it's a strain." We all chuckled.

Scott clapped Grandpa on the back, raised his thick brown eyebrows, and jerked a thumb towards me, "And are you keeping this one in line?" he asked.

"Well," Grandpa responded, "that's a struggle too, but we do our best."

Scott grinned, took off his green and white Co-op cap, and ran his hand through his short brown hair. We had agreed I would work for him part-time as needed, and he asked if I could help with stone picking that afternoon. "That back field is a mess of stones every spring and the day has arrived to tackle it, Sara. Can you be ready at one?"

"Sure," I said. "No problem."

Shortly before one o'clock I was dressed for picking stones—old jeans, t-shirt, sweat shirt, and hiking boots. Earlier, I had wrestled my hair into a high pony tail, crammed a baseball cap down on it, and eventually managed to thread the whole thing through the back opening of the cap. My hair was the colour of pale rust, and was very thick, naturally curly, and naturally out of control.

Just as I finished this hair accomplishment, Grandma walked by. "Sara you should really put on some sunscreen, you know you're as white as a ghost."

My heart skipped a beat at this particular comparison,

and I looked at her sharply, but she gave no sign of any covert meaning to her words. Sunscreen seemed a little overkill for the end of April, but I conceded and went to the entrance-way mirror to coat my face. As I smoothed the stuff on my paper-white skin, I decided she probably was right. My end-of-summer tan was generally the same colour as the rest of my family's skin in the middle of winter. There was a tiny sprinkling of freckles on my nose and cheeks, which would blossom into an abundant crop by mid-summer. As I made sure there were no white blobs on my face, Grandma came up beside me and gazed at me in the mirror.

"That's definitely better than getting a sunburn," she said. "I'm afraid you inherited your delicate skin from me."

"And the green parts of my eyes." I smiled at her in the mirror. My unusual eye colour was a combo of my Dad's brown eyes and Grandma's green, with some flecks of gold thrown in for good measure. "Dad calls them cat's eyes."

Grandma laughed and nodded.

With a water bottle and work gloves in hand, I sat out on the deck steps and waited for Scott. It was a refreshing, magnificent spring day. A red-winged black bird clung to a nearby swaying branch, while he sharply and repeatedly clarified his territory. In response to each statement, a similar call sounded-off from across the pond, but I was unsure if this was a rebuttal of agreement or dispute.

Right on time, Scott roared into the lane on a large no-

nonsense tractor. A little yellow Jeep soon zipped in behind, which was driven by a young guy I had never seen before.

Hmm, I thought to myself. *This could be interesting.*

Scott introduced me to Jesse, a university student who apparently was going to live and work at Stacy and Scott's place for the summer. Why had I not known about this before?! He had some tenuous connection to Scott—his sister's neighbour's son, or something along that line. I tried to appear studiously nonchalant as introductions were made, but my efforts may have been sabotaged by Jesse's wide smile and striking slate-blue eyes that triggered heart palpitations. I felt a blush creeping up my neck and face, but optimistically hoped my cap and the bright sunshine camouflaged it.

We spent all afternoon loading rocks into the megasized tractor bucket and dumping them into the edge of the bush, carrying on intermittent conversations, depending on the tractor noise and our proximity to each other.

Eventually, I couldn't help querying, "Where do all these stones come from every year? Do rocks grow from seeds and when they're finally big enough they rise to the surface?"

Jesse volunteered a second theory. "I'm thinking some of the neighbours get rid of their stones by dumping them here."

We laughed and eventually had a contest of shot-putting stones into the tractor bucket, which gave me an excellent chance to study Jesse. He was about the same height as Scott, a little less than six feet, but with a slimmer build. His face was sun-tanned already—or maybe it started out that way—and was framed by wayward sandy curls straggling out from the edges of a Blue Jays baseball cap. When you added in the contagious smile and those hypnotizing slate-blue eyes… well, some people might have called him adorable.

Scott randomly declared himself the shot-put winner, moved the tractor along, and then asked me, "So you're done your teacher training now, right? Have you applied for positions?"

"Yep," I said. "I am pleased to be officially finished school! I've applied to some school boards in the Toronto area, but haven't even gotten one response."

"Well, good luck," he said. "Something will come up somewhere, I expect. What about you, Jesse? What are you taking?"

"Electrical Engineering at York University," he replied. "I have one more year."

"Any ideas of where you'd like to work?"

"Not particularly. I'm thinking probably wherever I can get hired!"

A few minutes later, I came upon a large rock that was half buried in the ground and pointed it out to Jesse who was closest to me. He kicked dirt from around the edges with his work boots to assess the size, grabbed a pry bar from the tractor, worried away at the rock to loosen it, then wiggled the tool down underneath and pried it up about eight inches.

"Hey," he said to me, "see if you can stand on the end of the pry bar so I can pick up this brute."

This involved getting touchy-close to him and at one point, I put my hand on his shoulder for balance while he was still crouched down beside me. I felt another blush burning up my face, but thankfully he was looking at the rock. Then he let go of the pry bar and moved around across from me.

Somewhat surprisingly, I managed to keep my balance. Jesse grinned at me, said "Outstanding," then hunkered down in a squat, got his hands around the thing, and heaved. His lips clamped tightly together, his biceps bulged, and the veins on his neck stood out with the strain. By this time, Scott had brought the tractor up close to the activity, so when Jesse rose, he just pivoted and dropped the rock into the bucket.

"Well, that one wins the prize for the day," Scott said, and clapped Jesse on the back. "And I think we're done for now, about time we headed back for chores."

It had been an enjoyable afternoon out in the field... the heady smell of eager new growth, the balmy spring breeze against my face, the sunshine's promise of summer. It was soul cleansing. And Jesse still seemed... interesting.

That evening, I headed to my attic room at ten o'clock and snuggled down in bed with a book, pleasantly tired and reasonably optimistic about being undisturbed by ghosts or nightmares.

Earlier I had gone for a sunset walk, but unfortunately, the sunset was pretty much a bust. It started out promising, but demonstrated poor follow-through, and the finish was decidedly disappointing. I couldn't help but think it was rather similar to my love-life so far. The thing about sunsets though, is that you can be pretty sure you'll get another chance with one, and it might be outstanding. The optimist in me thought this could also be true of love. The rest of me sneered derisively, warning me not to get my hopes up about this Jesse guy. When I returned to the house after my walk, I complained to Grandma about both the sunset and my love life, (or lack thereof). She patted my hand and made me a cup of tea with honey.

Chapter Four

Over the next few days I sent out applications to a few more school boards; Guelph and Kitchener areas mainly, although I was not feeling optimistic about the results.

I also helped Grandpa clean the main cellar of the old house (bigger, but it had less junk in it than the little cellar), and then we borrowed Stacy and Scott's truck and took two loads to the dump. And when I say dump, I mean an actual dump, not a "Waste Management Site." This was the dumpiest dump I ever hoped to see. Hills and mountains and valleys of junk and garbage.

The most interesting part of the dump run was going into Scott and Stacy's place afterwards to exchange the truck for Grandpa's van. Their black and white border collie, Buzz (as in Buzz Lightyear), loudly announced our arrival, resulting in Scott and Jesse emerging from the implement shed. Trailing behind them was a calico cat, which I immediately scooped up for a cuddle.

"She's got four kittens in the barn if you want to go see them," said Scott.

"I sure would," I replied. "Where are they?"

"I'll show you," Jesse offered, and we headed to the barn. It was mid-afternoon and the cows were outside, so we strode by the empty stalls to the far side of the downstairs, and behind a barrier of small straw bales, the kittens tumbled together in a playful heap. I awed and oohed and picked each one up in turn.

"I made this little corral to keep them away from the cows, but it won't be long until they can get out," Jesse said, as he stroked the heads of two kittens at a time. "But hopefully they're smart enough by then to keep out from underfoot."

"Do they have names?" I asked.

"Oh yes, the kids named them, of course. I think this one is Simba, this one Nala, then there's Zazu and Pumbaa."

Laughing out loud, I said, "So most of the Lion King cast, in other words."

"Yep, although I might have Pumbaa and Zazu mixed up." He grinned at me and my heart sped up a tick.

Grandpa was waiting in the van so we headed home, and then I strolled around the pond and contemplated Jesse. I also pondered the perfect reflections of upside down trees on the surface of the water. Their symmetry was almost hypnotic. Jesse was a bit entrancing too, but I didn't want to be tricked into thinking he was a nice guy if he actually wasn't. But he really seemed so great!

After supper, the sunset was cheerful and affirmative—a panorama of colours which later faded and left behind piles of pale pink clouds, like mountains of cotton candy on the horizon. I took it as a good sign. Who doesn't like cotton candy?

That night, I went to sleep smiling, and woke up the next morning feeling optimistic. As always, I surveyed my room for uninvited guests, but it was the fifth day in a row without any creepy, heart-stopping sightings or nightmares. Alright then.

The weather, however, didn't really match my mood. It was cold and soggy out. I sat with Grandma and Grandpa at the table in the big room, finishing breakfast and gazing out the wet window. The clouds were low and spilling over, and the willows drooped in despair. But Grandma had started a small fire in the fireplace "to chase the damp away," and the room felt cozy and glad.

"Sara," Grandpa said. "Could you go upstairs and bring down the two cardboard boxes in the hall closet?"

"Sure," I said and headed out the room.

There was so much in the boxes to admire and sort through that we didn't even get through the first one that day. It contained a scattering of knickknacks and old jewelry, along with shoeboxes and envelopes full of photos. Grandma and Grandpa reminisced all morning, telling me stories from their childhood and the war time. It was fabulous.

There was an amazing picture of a baby-faced Grandpa, just past his eighteenth birthday, in his World War II air force uniform, standing in front of a plane. He was a flight instructor during the war and spent most of it stationed in various places across Canada.

My favourite picture of Grandma showed her sitting cross legged in the middle of an orchard eating an apple. Grandma gazed at the picture with memory eyes. The camera had captured the most beautiful smile as long wavy hair tumbled over her shoulders.

"How old would you be then, Grandma?" I asked.

"16 or 17, I guess, around the beginning of the war, when Racheal and I picked apples over Meaford way one fall."

"I guess I got my curly hair from you," I said, and she nodded and smiled.

It was a black and white picture, but Grandpa informed me that Grandma's hair had earned her the nickname "Red" in her younger days.

"It was a brighter red than your hair," he said. "Kind of like the red in the coals of a campfire after it has died down. And she has always been a fiery one too!" he added, putting his hand on her shoulder. "Isn't that right, dear?"

Grandma teased back. "Well, someone had to keep

you in line!" Then she reached out and ran her hand down the back of my head. "And my hair used to be thick like yours," she said, letting a big chunk of hair slide through her hand. "Not like the way it is now, that's for sure," and she patted her white, permed curls with disdain.

After lunch, Grandma and I stayed at the table looking at photos while Grandpa elected to read his book on the couch. Eventually, Grandma found a photo of about ten adults standing in front of an old shed and placed her index finger on a lady she described as my Grandpa's Aunt Agnes, Sadie's sister.

"Agnes had some issues" she said. "Now-a-days it would be called mental health issues, but back then people generally just shook their heads and called her crazy. Not to her face, mind you."

Instantly alert and wary I asked, "What do you mean *crazy*. What did she do?"

"Well, mostly she seemed pretty normal, but she had a couple quirks. The thing I remember most was this routine she had of climbing out the side kitchen window, walking around the house, and going in through the back door. She had to do this three times in a row, I think two or three times a day, and neither rain, nor snow, nor sleet held her back. Being just kids, when we walked by her place coming or going to school, we were always on the look-out for this little spectacle, and giggled behind the roadside bushes while we watched."

"Do you remember anything else?" I asked.

"Well, she always repeated a girl's name while she

went through her routine, and looked around like she was searching for something… or someone. What was that name?" she asked herself, tapping the picture on the table. "What was it now? I should remember—I spied on her enough." Then she called over to Grandpa. "Eugene, what was the name that Aunt Agnes used to repeat when she did her little routine?"

Grandpa slowly looked up from his book. "You mean out the window and around the house?"

Grandma confirmed this and he thoughtfully placed his bookmark in the book, closed it up in slow motion, and set it on the coffee table. He rose from the couch and shuffled towards the table, eyes pondering the floor, deep in thought, glasses sliding down his nose.

"I think it's coming 'round on the rolodex," he mused, as he lowered himself onto the chair at the end of the table. When he landed, he looked straight at me. "Oh," he said, "I know… it was Sara. Sara was the name she said."

As he spoke, something that felt rather like an electric shock zipped up my spine and caused me to shudder.

Grandma concurred. "Sara! Of course, that was it. I should have been able to think of that!" But she had noticed me shiver. "Ghost walk over your grave?" she asked.

Looking at her with blank alarm, I managed to blurt out, "What?"

"It was a saying the old folks used when someone had a shiver for no reason."

"But it makes no sense," I pointed out a little shakily, "since I'm clearly alive and don't have a grave."

"You're right," she agreed. "I never thought it made any sense either. I guess now that I'm an old folk, I should put an end to its use."

I forced out a little laugh but felt quite perturbed by the whole weird conversation. So my great, great (and crazy) aunt had been looking for someone with my name. Huh.

That night, the coffin nightmare tormented me again. I woke up my heart hammering, drenched in a cold sweat. Going back to sleep was not an option, so finally, as the first hint of morning light seeped through the windows, I threw on some clothes, sprinted down two flights of stairs, and went out to greet the day.

A pair of geese flapped across the brightening sky, with the gander needlessly honking instructions to his mate. I watched until they were only specks in the distance. Then, after a couple deep breaths of cool morning air, on impulse I started running towards the barn and beyond. It felt like the right way to purge Rasputin from my mind and soul. By the time I was past the first field my mood had lifted, my mind had cleared, and my body seemed to be celebrating the movement. So I decided right then and there to start running regularly again.

By the time I got back to the house, a gusty wind was whipping my hair around and the tree branches were dancing. Ominous clouds battled with the early morning light.

During breakfast, large rain drops began plopping against the windows.

Grandma and I decided to finish looking through the first box from the upstairs closet, but Grandpa said, "Reckon I should work on that golf cart. I'll clean up all the terminals and check the connections." The golf cart—housed in the garage—was refusing to charge, and he knew Grandma would soon be anxious to drive back the farm lane to monitor the crop growth.

After I brought the box to the table, there was more rummaging and reminiscing. We found an adorable little flowered sugar bowl that Grandma said I could keep. There was a box of old English coins and a couple brooches. There were lots of photos too, mostly black and white. Grandma picked up a picture of teenaged Grandpa, with a younger brother and their mom, Sadie, all weeding a vegetable garden. Grandma explained that Grandpa eventually had two younger half-brothers, and also a half-sister.

"How old would Sadie—or should I say Gran—have been in this picture? And what happened to her first husband?" I asked, studying the photo.

"Well, according to your Grandpa's age, Sadie was probably about 40 in this photo."

"What!?" I exclaimed, "She looks so much older than that!"

"Yes, I agree, but Gran had a hard life. Only months after they married, her first husband was killed on the streets of Montreal while trying to stop a runaway horse and wagon. Gran was already pregnant… with your grand-father. She moved to Toronto and supported herself and the baby by working long hours in a boarding house for a few years while taking care of the child. Then she married again, probably thinking that she couldn't continue to manage on her own, but by marrying Cecil, she really jumped out of the frying pan and into the fire."

I raising my eyebrows. "What do you mean?"

"Well, I'm not sure she was any better off, marrying a man like that. Eventually, your grandfather had two younger half brothers and a younger half sister. But Cecil was a mean, nasty fellow… particularly towards Gran and Eugene. Anyway, that was a long time ago now."

Clearly, Grandma was closing that topic, so I picked up a black and white school photo of twelve kids plus a male teacher standing in front of a one-room school house with a small chalkboard sign that read S. S. # 6, Glenelg Lorriston. I must say, they were a pretty tough looking bunch. "When would this have been taken?" I asked.

"Oh, I guess that would have been 1931 or '32."

Nodding, I studied the old photo. Growing up in the Great Depression had been serious business, as proven by the children's somber thin faces and tattered clothes. I couldn't help thinking that these twelve young people had gazed at the camera as if it were their future, as if they knew what was coming. Less than a decade later, they would trade in the poverty of childhood for the hardships and horror of war.

Pointing to a little girl in the front row, I asked, "Is that you, Grandma?" The child had chin length hair pulled tight off her forehead and tucked behind her ears, and she wore a dress that had clearly belonged to others before her. She peered towards the camera with a solemn expression that looked slightly accusing. After a few more minutes, I found Grandpa, who was a head taller than Grandma, and had a shock of thick wavy hair falling across his forehead.

Grandma laughed and said, "Eugene and his family moved into the area when I was in grade two and he went into grade four. We all thought it was so funny that Eugene and his younger brother wore long socks and short pants to school… English style. Of course that was all Gran knew. It only lasted a year, and then I guess the boys revolted." Grandma then pointed to a boy next to her in the photo. "That was Tom, your Grandpa's cousin, oldest son of the woman who did the 'round the house' routine. He was a troubled boy… sometimes he was very lively and great fun to be around, but on many days he was angry with the world and refused to talk or to do any school work. When he was a teenager, he and a couple other young fellows went west, "riding the rails" as many did in the dirty thirties, looking for work and adventure, bumming for food. But some months later, word came back that Tom was killed by a train."

"Oh, how awful," I said.

Grandma continued to look at the photo thoughtfully. "A few years later, one of the friends who was with him, told me that Tom "lost his mind" and jumped in front of that train on purpose. Apparently, Tom was yelling, "Leave me alone! Get away!" just before he jumped, but he wasn't talking to his friends and no one else was around. I don't know, maybe it was some kind of seizure or something."

Grandma put a finger on a girl in the front row of the photo. "This is Martha, Tom's younger sister, so your Grandpa's cousin too. We still keep in touch with her, but it's been a while since we've talked. I should give her a call this week."

Chapter Five

The first Monday in May was hot, sunny, and glorious. Grandpa went into the Co-op farm-supply store and brought back twelve bags of mulch, and I spent the day mulching the various flower beds, while he puttered about cutting down old flower stalks and getting the outside water working. It felt great to wear summer clothes with the warm sunshine heating up my back.

Just after lunch, I was caught off guard when Jesse arrived by tractor with a folded-up disc attached. He stopped, gave me a once over with those eyes, and seemingly hid some private joke behind a smile. My tangled ponytail was a mess, I probably had garden dirt on my face, and I'm pretty sure I blushed.

"Scott said to ask if you could drive me back before supper, as he wants the tractor and disc left here overnight."

Of course I said yes.

When Jesse returned from the field at five o'clock, I was all cleaned up, having spent a ridiculous half-hour belabouring over what to wear for this five-minute drive down the road. Anyway, I ended up in my best jeans and a forest green shirt.

We climbed into my 1996 Honda Civic, a hand-me-down from my mom. Actually, first I had to clear the socks, sweatshirt, winter boots, and Tim Horton's garbage from the passenger seat. I should have cleaned up the car earlier.

"Sorry, my car generally looks like a bedroom threw up in it."

Jesse laughed and shook his head.

On the short drive, Jesse asked about responses to my job applications (there had been none) and queried whether I'd investigated jobs in the Grey-Bruce area. It was an interesting idea, and one I had not previously considered.

When we arrived at my cousin's farm, Stacy was just getting home from teaching at the high school in town. She had picked up their two kids from the after-school babysitter and they tumbled out of the car and raced towards Jesse and I. Buzz charged in a blur from the direction of the barn, barked wildly, and greeted everyone with riotous, overwhelming joy. I gave each kid a twirl around and Jesse in turn held each one upside down while Buzz licked their faces (yuck), resulting in much shrieking and laughter.

Stacy shook her head and laughed at the silliness, then said, "It's such a nice afternoon, we should have the season's first beer on the deck."

Jesse responded with an enthusiastic "Outstanding," and I was quick to agree.

Stacy went into the house and shortly returned with four beers, wearing jeans and a red t-shirt. She was a bit taller than I, quite slim, and had brown, medium length hair which she had pulled back into a short ponytail. She texted Scott who quickly emerged from the barn having just finished the afternoon milking. He trundled up the deck steps, elicited hugs from his children, set his stained Massey Ferguson cap on the deck railing, and settled happily into a chair. We all had a couple beers while taking turns playing soccer in front of the deck with 7-year-old Brandon, who had an exhausting supply of energy. Buzz was pretty good at soccer too, although he was a bit of a ball-hog.

4-year-old Maggie sat on the deck beside us, engrossed in making name cards for the two house cats, Salt and Pepper. Stacy had a CD playing from the kitchen window sill, and Maggie took regular dance breaks when the beat moved her, bursting to her feet and twirling and jumping, blonde pigtails flying. "Dance with me, Sara!" she pleaded, dragging me up to join her, and half-way through my second beer, I think I stopped blushing. After Maggie glued the final sparkles in place, the name cards were mounted over the cat's dishes in the kitchen, with much fanfare (from the adults, not the cats).

Stacy insisted I stay for dinner. Afterwards, Jesse, myself, and the kids played a hilarious game of Hungry Hippo. When Stacy hauled the kids off for baths, Jesse and Scott headed out to the barn to finish the feeding, and I drove back down the road to Grandma and Grandpa's.

Before going into the farmhouse, I walked around the pond to monitor the sunset and ponder Jesse. He was great with the kids and they clearly adored him. It was a fun evening… with maybe more to come? I gazed westward and was mesmerized by clouds of sapphire feather-dusters that swept across the high western sky. Down below, blankets of indigo and peach draped over the horizon. It was a calm, serene sunset. *Maybe a hopeful one,* I thought.

The following morning, I came downstairs dressed in proper gear to embark on some serious running, but when Grandpa saw me he warned, "There was frost on the ground earlier this morning. The temperature really dropped. You might want to re-think your get-up."

Heeding his advice, a jacket, gloves, and headband were added to my ensemble. The day before, I had worn shorts… such is spring-time in Canada. At the end of the lane, I turned south towards the hamlet of Scone, about two kilometres away, and quickly got into a rhythm.

My body, mind, and soul felt completely energized by

the exercise and fresh air, and I suddenly realized that country living agreed with me. The city was like an over-crowded, overheated room where everyone yells to make themselves heard. I hated the noise, the congestion, the stupid drivers... especially the stupid drivers. Although I hadn't actually resorted (yet) to jumping out of my car and banging a snow scraper on someone's front hood, fantasies had occurred. The farm, however, had a calming affect on me, and I decided to investigate potential teaching jobs in Grey and Bruce counties.

About halfway to Scone, I met an Amish horse and buggy and gave the occupants a jaunty wave. The man waved back and smiled, but the woman appeared deeply critical of my outfit, my swinging ponytail, and my activi-ty. Not allowing this cold-shoulder to disrupt my positive mood, I maintained my rhythm and a few minutes later, pounded over the Scone bridge in triumph.

Slowing to a walk, I circumnavigated the old one-room schoolhouse, which was the main feature in the ham-let of Scone. The little red-bricked building was used as a community centre—card parties, meetings, and family re-unions in the summer. My mom had actually attended the schoolhouse until grade six, after which it was closed down and the pupils bussed to a central school in town. The Saugeen River flowed along the edge of the property and apparently, during winter school days, there was a skating rink on the river, used at noon hours, which I ex-pect gave the teacher nightmares.

My mom once told me about twenty-five kids had attended Scone school with her, twice the number as in the photo of Grandma and Grandpa's school days. My mind shifted to Grandpa's teenage cousin who jumped in front of a train, yelling at someone to leave him alone. Abruptly, I stopped walking and gazed out over the river. The boy's friends had claimed no one was there, so who or what had Tom seen... a vision, a hallucination, a ghost? I squinted my eyes at some geese swimming in the water, and tried to remember something else Grandma said about Tom. Oh yes, he had extreme mood changes. Then it struck me... could Tom have had bi-polar disorder? Could bi-polar disorder cause hallucinations? It was Tom's mother who did the out-the-window, around-the-house routine... while calling *my* name. She couldn't actually have been looking for me, could she? No, of course not, Sara has always been a popular name. Still, there were several disturbing facts about that family... about my ancestors.

Rounding the front of the schoolhouse, I stopped and took a couple big breaths to clear my head. A robin started running towards me in short, indecisive spurts, but after one last dash, he threw me a suspicious look and flew off in the opposite direction. I took off too, retracing my steps back over the bridge toward home. When I met another horse and buggy, my wave and "good morning" was greeted with a lifting-of-the-reins acknowledgement from the man, and a lovely smile from the woman, who apparently was fairly accepting of the strange habits of the non-Amish.

Chapter Six

On a rainy morning a couple days later, I sat at the table with Grandma, nursing a second cup of tea while bemoaning the fact that once again Raving Rasputin had disrupted my sleep during the previous night.

"His rants usually involve Bible quotes," I said, watching the willows bow down with the weight of the rain. "Or what I take as Bible quotes." (My Bible knowledge was fairly sketchy.) "Things like, 'who despised the word of the Lord by doing evil in His sight,' and something about the 'voice of your sister's blood crying from the ground,' and at times, something about a mother of nations. I've written down as much as I remember—he tends to repeat himself a lot."

"Maybe you should search online and figure out if they are really Bible quotes," suggested Grandma.

That thought had crossed my mind more than once; but truthfully, the idea frightened me. What if they actually were direct quotes from the Bible… in the dreams of someone who has never read the Bible?

"But other times," I continued, "his ravings don't seem so Biblical. He repeats 'my princess' a lot, as in 'my radiant princess,' and something about her whiteness and her hands. I just don't get it. Oh, and he often yells about 'too many children!' and 'so many mouths to feed!' That doesn't sound very Biblical, does it?"

Glancing at Grandma, I realized with a start that she was staring at me with her cup suspended half way between the table and her mouth. With a shaking hand, she slowly set down the cup. Some tea sloshed over the side, but she didn't seem to notice. She stared at me with lips clamped tightly together.

"Grandma?" I queried nervously.

She shook her head a bit, cleared her throat, then noticed the spilled tea and carefully wiped it up with her napkin. She stared at the table and the pit of my stomach told me there was something to dread.

"Grandma, are you alright?"

She cleared her throat again, and a third time, and then finally met my eyes. "Your Uncle Ray…" she whispered, and the words hung in the space between us. Her lips moved a bit more but no sound came out. There was sorrow in her eyes.

And the knowledge, the memory, the understanding, suddenly crashed down on me. "Uncle Ray!" I cried out, and she knew that I knew.

Grandma and Grandpa's son Ray, was in his early forties and had suffered from schizophrenia since his late teens. He lived in a group home in Owen Sound where I had gone to visit him many times with Mom. He attended family gatherings in his younger years, but he was unpredictable since crowds—and particularly small children—upset him. It was better if he visited with only a couple people at a time. When I was just a kid, Ray had become very upset during a big Thanksgiving gathering at the farmhouse. He yelled over and over, "Too many children!", "Too many mouths to feed!" and "There's never enough food!" At the time I thought this was quite strange since the tables were loaded down with a feast. Grandma and Grandpa had taken Ray upstairs to calm him and we children were told not to go upstairs. Ray didn't come down for the rest of the day, and that was probably the last time he was involved with a large family gathering.

Taking a big breath, I blurted out my worst fear, the fear that had been twisting inside me for weeks. "Grandma, do you think I have schizophrenia?"

"No!" she said emphatically. "But..." and she stared at me while her eyes grew greener with unshed tears. "But I wonder..." she whispered, "if you can figure out these dreams... what they mean or something... I wonder if maybe it might help your Uncle Ray?"

Later that morning, with Ray on their minds, Grandma and Grandpa decided to visit him, and I opted to join them. Grandpa had phoned ahead and when we arrived at the group home Uncle Ray was sitting on one of the front porch chairs. He was a tall, slim man, with short dark hair, and a timid, serious nature. He was dressed in khaki pants, burgundy golf shirt, and a navy spring jacket, and as usual, seemed uncomfortable with the world. His green eyes were like Grandma's, but those eyes always looked wary and wounded, which considering the schizophrenia, was understandable. Although Ray stood when we went up the porch stairs, he did not offer a greeting or a smile.

Grandma gave him a brief hug, which was not reciprocated, and said, "Look, Sara came for a visit too."

Smiling, I said, "Hi Uncle Ray. I haven't seen you for awhile."

He didn't make eye contact or say anything, but he nodded slightly.

Grandpa put his hand on Ray's shoulder. "So son, where would you like to go for lunch? Maybe the Chinese buffet, or we could go to the restaurant at the harbour, or that Italian place downtown. What do you think?"

Ray responded with, "Chinese," and immediately headed towards the car.

During lunch, Grandma, Grandpa, and I updated Ray about farm and family happenings, but it was difficult to tell if he was interested or not. When Ray was asked a question, he either provided very brief replies, or did not answer at all. Thankfully, the restaurant was buffet-style, and the getting up and sitting down helped relieve the strained conversation, somewhat.

None-the-less, I felt relief when lunch was over and Uncle Ray was deposited back at the group home. As we drove through more rain, I found myself feeling guilty and sad. Ray had been robbed of a normal life, and quite likely a regular man was hiding behind that stilted, awkward guy at lunch. I vowed to make an effort to visit him more frequently, no matter how uncomfortable and awkward it seemed.

But there was something else. Even though I tried to block it, my mind kept circling back to the real possibility of myself descending down the same menacing, heart-rending road as my Uncle Ray, and apparently other family members before him. Grandma looked back at me just as I involuntarily shuddered.

"There's a little blanket on the other seat if you're cold, dear," she said. I nodded and pulled over the blanket.

That evening, I sat on my bed and conferred with my sister Beth during our weekly Skype visit. My sister was three years older than me. She and her husband lived and worked in downtown Toronto. Despite our considerable differences in personalities and lifestyles, we had become pretty close over the last several months. Prior to that, we were definitely not close. Since the turbulent teenage years, we had continued to brace ourselves against each other. Not that we actually fought, it just seemed that whenever we were together, we both raised up invisible shields between us. All interactions were guarded, stilted, laden with suspicion and negative undertones. Then, during a big farm family event a year ago last September, I had an epiphany.

According to Google, epiphany means, *"a sudden, intuitive perception of, or insight into the reality or essential meaning of something, usually initiated by some simple, homely, or commonplace occurrence or experience."* Yep, that is what I had—an epiphany.

It started when I was in the big farm kitchen helping with meal prep. My mom and her sister, Alice, were cleaning potatoes and wrapping them in foil while they invented silly toasts, clicking their wine glasses together with much fanfare and laughing over family stories, old and new. While ripping up lettuce for a salad, it hit me, I wanted that kind of friendship with my sister. I wanted it then, and also at my mom's age and beyond. I wanted that easy, comfortable relationship, those shared experiences, that connection.

Later that evening, as the gang sat around the campfire at the pond lawn, I watched my grandmother and her sister chatting and laughing. Grandma's sister from the neighbouring farm sipped a beer, while Grandma had her hands wrapped around a cup of tea. They somehow started talking about making maple syrup when they were kids. With their older sister and brother, they were sent back to the bush with the horse to gather the sap and boil it down in the sugar shack.

Everyone around the campfire enjoyed the reminiscing, and again it struck me… I wanted that. I gazed across the flames at my sister who had our cousin's little daughter on her knee, and was trying to show her the Big Dipper in the star-filled night sky. Really, why couldn't we have that kind of relationship? I decided we could, but one of us would have to throw away our invisible shield and take the first step. And that someone would be me.

Standing up, I asked if there were any requests from the kitchen, then headed on a beer and wine run. In the darkness between the campfire and the house, I crossed over to the front lawn which was well out of the campfire viewing range. I stood in the middle of the night-filled lawn and pantomimed ripping off that stupid invisible shield and throwing it on the ground. I stomped on it vigorously, and finally drop-kicked that thing clear across the County Line. Then, squaring my shoulders and dusting the invisible dirt off my hands, I turned around to see the full moon just peeking over the top of the house.

"Hello Moon," I said, and grinned up at it. "We can do it, you just watch us."

After punting my shield, I was amazed that Beth seemed to tentatively lower hers as well. At first, she responded cautiously and a bit suspiciously to my increased interest in her opinions and her life, but she had definitely warmed up to me over the last several months. She had even invited me to Toronto to help celebrate her birthday in January and we had a great weekend.

Anyway, the evening after lunch with Uncle Ray, my sister and I were having our regular Skype visit which included me telling her about yet another Rasputin nightmare from the previous evening.

"I'm so sorry your nightmares started harassing you at the farm, Sara. I was hoping that staying there would block them entirely."

"Yeah, I was kind of hoping for that too, but no such luck. Grandma says I should research whether Rasputin's ravings are actually from the Bible, but I'm really nervous to find out. You know I've never read the Bible, so what if it turns out his ravings are actual quotes? That would be too much to handle."

I was unprepared and completely flabbergasted (such a great word...flabbergasted) by what Beth said next. "Well, why don't you send me the wording of Rasputin's rants and I'll figure them out. You know I'm coming up next weekend anyway, so I'll share the results with you then. At least that way you won't be by yourself."

Beth's offer was a big relief but I was still quite apprehensive. We said goodbye and then, to clear my head, I galloped down the two sets of stairs and through the front door to check out the sunset. It had stopped raining. Heavy grey clouds packed the western sky, except for a wide horizontal band of vibrant orange and coral along the horizon. But by the time I walked around the pond, the swelling clouds had squeezed the colour into a narrow, horizontal strip like a fiery orange eye-mask peering through the haze. Gradually that strip shrunk and shrunk, and then, as if a switch had been thrown, it was gone, with only sullen grey left behind.

Chapter Seven

On Saturday, Beth arrived around noon and we had lunch in the porch with Grandma and Grandpa. There had been intermittent rain and drizzle during the morning, but it was still warm and we were glad to be breathing in the springness. My sister had thick chestnut hair cut in a short asymmetrical style, with a crown of long bangs sweeping across her forehead. She was tall and slim (I think her legs went up to my waist), and I knew from my January visit in Toronto that when Beth dressed up in a suit and heels, she looked every bit the part of a downtown young executive.

In the afternoon, Beth and I sat cross-legged on my bed with her laptop and some printed pages in between us.

While a steady sound of drops pattered on the skylight above, Beth locked her brown eyes onto my hazel ones.

"Little sister," she said, "brace yourself."

My heart sped up and I took a big breath.

"Several of the things Rasputin says in your night-mares are, in fact, in the Bible… word for word. I don't know how that is possible or what it means." She studied my face.

I wasn't sure whether to feel intrigued or horrified, perhaps both mixed-up together. Beth handed me some printed pages and read out loud from her laptop. She had determined that Rasputin's ravings appeared to come from the following Bible verses:

Exodus 23:7: *Keep far from a false charge, and do not kill the innocent and righteous, for I will not acquit the wicked.*

Samuel 12:9: *'Why have you despised the word of the Lord by doing evil in his sight?'*

Psalms 106:38: *'And shed innocent blood, the blood of their sons and their daughters, whom they sacrificed to the idols of Canaan; And the land was polluted with the blood.'*

Isaiah 57:5: *'Who inflame yourselves among the oaks, under every luxuriant tree. Who slaughter the children in the ravines, under the clefts of the crags?'*

Genesis 4:10-11: *'What have you done? The voice of your brother's blood is crying to Me from the ground. Now you are cursed from the ground, which has opened its mouth to receive your brother's blood from your hand.'*

Pretty heavy stuff, Rasputin.

"And as if the whole thing is not weird enough," my sister added, "bizarrely, in that last quote, Rasputin changed the word brother to sister, as in '*to receive your sister's blood from your hand.*'" She rubbed both hands over her face and then gazed at me, "I just don't know what to say, Sara."

"So my brain conjured up accurate bits of Bible verses, although I've never read the Bible, then made that one little change?" We stared at each other with eyes wide and several minutes passed in silence.

Finally, I whispered, "Beth, am I going crazy? Is this the kind of thing that happens when people lose their minds? Am I going to end up like Uncle Ray?"

It almost seemed as though Beth had been ready for that question and answered immediately. "No, Sara, you're not going crazy. These quotes have been conveyed to you somehow. You did not just invent accurate Bible quotes! But what if you have some kind of extra perception that's connecting you to another dimension somehow?"

"Another dimension? I don't even know what that means."

"What if Rasputin and the little girl are reaching out to you for a reason, to give you some kind of message perhaps, or maybe they need your help somehow?"

"Beth that makes no sense. How can I help someone who is in my nightmares?"

"Well…" She paused. "What if, once upon a time, the little girl and Rasputin were real people?"

We locked eyes, and my heart revved up.

Beth took a big breath and continued. "I've read that sometimes when people die they have trouble moving into the next dimension. Something holds them back. It could be that something was left unfinished. Maybe this is an attempt by Rasputin and the little girl to make contact with our dimension."

"Well, if you're right, I sincerely wish they would contact someone else. And anyway, there's also the coffin nightmare, how would that fit in?"

"I don't know how it all goes together, but it has to mean something, Sara. Rasputin accurately quoting the Bible is not just some wild coincidence."

It was impossible to get my head around Beth's theories. In the end, the only obvious conclusion was that the whole situation was getting weirder and weirder.

Chapter Eight

*B*eth headed back to the city on Sunday, and the following morning I woke up to rain splattering on the skylight above my bed. Grandma, Grandpa, and I decided it was a good day to look through the second cardboard box from the upstairs closet.

At the top of the box was a folder containing some faded documents. To my amazement, there was a recommendation letter given to Great Grandma Sadie from the A. & W. Flatau & Co, Shoe Manufacturers. It was dated August 17, 1920, with the company name on the top of the page in elaborate curly letters. Beneath was a pen and ink sketch of the factory and the following typed note:

To whom it may concern.

This is to certify that (Miss) Sadie Hall of 29, Earlesmead Road, Tottenham, N17., who was apprenticed to us upon leaving school, has been in our employ (working on the Hand Method Folding Machine) for 10 years.

She has proved an excellent worker, proficient, industrious, punctual, very reliable and regular in attendance, and we can highly recommend her for any situation of a similar character.

She is leaving us to go abroad, and we are very sorry to lose her.

The letter was signed by a K. Cohen, who apparently was the Works Manager. And there was also a little pink folded pamphlet that identified Great Grandma as a *Woman Member of The London Metropolitan Branch of the National Union of Boot and Shoe Operatives, 1919-1920*, with a Union Registered Number of 105421, at Branch Number 296. (I loved that it was pink.)

After the exciting discovery of these documents, we sifted through some photos and found a small picture of Great Grandma Sadie's wedding.

"Grandma, it looks like a pretty solemn affair, doesn't it?" Great Grandma Sadie looked stoic, while her new husband, Cecil, looked positively grim.

"Well, I think Sadie knew it was going to be a tough life, but hoped it was better than being a single mom."

I pulled out a large oval frame from the bottom of the box and to my delight, it was Grandma and Grandpa's wedding picture.

"Grandma, this is beautiful!"

She wore a pale, knee-length dress, with three-quarter sleeves, a high v-neckline, and had a large, heart-shaped locket around her neck. Her hair was rolled back off her face at the front, as was the fashion, and long, curly tresses tumbled past her shoulders. The black and white photo was accented with some hand-colouring, pale pink on their cheeks, some brightness on Grandma's lips, and just enough tint in her hair to suggest redness. Grandpa looked handsome and self-assured in his air-force uniform, but that baby-face could have belonged to a 15-year old kid! He had one arm around Grandma, who was leaning into him. It was a stunning picture of them both.

"How old were you, Grandma?"

"Well, we grew up fast in those days," she said. "Didn't have a choice really." I raised my eyebrows at her and repeated the question. With pursed lips and a slight gleam in her eye, she glanced at Grandpa. "It was six weeks past my eighteenth birthday."

Laughing, I said, "It seems that you knew what you were doing, since it's lasted sixty-three years and counting! So Grandpa, you were 20 then, right?"

"I turned 20 two weeks after we were married."

"You should have this hanging up somewhere," I said, and after some further persuasion and a tour of possible locations, Grandpa installed the picture in the entranceway.

Excellent. With that accomplished, we returned to the box for a few more minutes and I found another wedding picture, which apparently was of Grandpa's Aunt Agnes... Sadie's sister.

"So Grandma, were there any other weird things Agnes did besides her "out the window" routine?"

"Well, we keep in touch with her daughter Martha, and a few years ago she mentioned that when she was a kid, her mother was very unpredictable, with huge swings in her personality and mood. The children never knew what to expect from her. Oh, I still haven't called Martha. I'll do it this afternoon."

At supper time Grandma reported that Martha would be coming to the farm for a visit. "Apparently, she was sorting through some old boxes of her mother's a while ago, and found several diaries that belonged to your Grandpa's mother, Sadie. Martha has no idea how they came to be amongst Sadie's sister's stuff, but Martha is coming for lunch next Tuesday and will bring them with her."

"Grandma, that's amazing!" I exclaimed.

"Should be interesting," agreed Grandma, "I don't remember your Grandpa's mother ever saying that she kept a diary when she was young."

Chapter Nine

There were two more days of rain, and then the third morning arrived like a sunny spring gift. When I got up at eight o'clock, the house was empty, so I wandered out the back door, looked around, and smiled at the transformation. The countryside seemed to actually beam with satisfaction and pride about its freshly-greened self. Grandma and Grandpa were inspecting the new sprouts in the big perennial garden, with Grandma sitting on a stool, directing Grandpa about which green things were weeds and which would magically turn into irises, peonies, and hollyhock.

"We have green grass!" I exclaimed and they nodded and laughed.

"Yep," said Grandpa. "Another few days and your grandmother will be wanting it cut. She's just never satisfied," he teased, "she wants the darn stuff to grow but then wants to mow it down."

The ancient apple tree towards the barn was covered with pink and white blossoms, and I walked over to breathe in the fresh, delicate sweetness. The birch tree, monarch of the lawns, still refused to show signs of life. As though hurrying was beneath her station in life, she would be the last to show her spring beauty. The willows were the front runners, with leafy branches hanging gracefully like long locks of hair.

"Grandma, do you think you can supervise two at a time?" I asked.

She agreed, but insisted I have some breakfast first, so I scrambled inside and returned with one of Grandma's home-made muffins, a bowl of applesauce, and a piece of cheese. Once I finished, I tip-toed carefully into the new greenery to help out, and after about an hour, the garden was in pretty good shape. Grandpa and I spent a couple more hours on the lawns that day, gathering up more sticks and branches. Once the tractor bucket was full, Grandpa headed out to dump it back the lane while I moved on to the next area. At two o'clock, I explained that I was off the clock for the day.

"In about an hour, Jesse has to go to Owen Sound to pick up a replacement part for the hay mower and he invited me to go with him. We're going out for dinner." There were nods and smiles and some twinkling eyes as I headed for the shower.

We were going for dinner at the Harbour Inn overlooking the water, and I was mildly ecstatic about our first actual date. Well, I thought it was a date anyway. At four o'clock, the little yellow Jeep zipped into the lane and I bounced down the outside steps. After struggling with wardrobe decisions again, I settled on black jeans, a royal blue shirt, and carried a denim jacket. My hair was somewhat tamed by a black hairband.

While climbing in, I smiled at Jesse and said, "Yellow is an interesting choice."

"Well, sometimes a person needs to make a statement, you know?" he said. "Stand out in the crowd. Also she was a really good price, probably because she was yellow." While I was laughing, he backed the Jeep towards the garage to turn around, then paused to look at me. "Have you ever been told you have a killer smile?"

Tossing off another one, I replied, "Well, I have now."

"Outstanding," he said, grinning, then shifted into first gear and drove out the lane.

Looking around, I was amused by the extreme tidiness of the interior of the Jeep. Dashes and windows were shiny, floor mats were free of dirt and grass. There was a ball cap on the backseat and that was it. Nothing else.

"Wow, I'm impressed... so clean and tidy. My car is

such a mess."

Jesse laughed. "Little Miss Sunshine and I have a mutual respect for each other. I take care of her and she takes care of me."

"Little Miss Sunshine?" I queried with a laugh.

"Well, I usually just call her Missy," he said.

Returning to the farm at eight-thirty, I walked around the pond to monitor the day's growth and the sunset. The trees actually looked greener than they had first thing that morning. Before going in the house, I took a last look at the western sky. A wide band of baby-girl pink sat on the horizon, while above it stretched an endless expanse of robin egg blue… like infinite possibilities.

Grandma greeted me in the kitchen with a poorly concealed grin. "Well, how was your evening?"

Trying to downplay my excitement, I casually said, "Oh, it was fun. We sat on the outside patio at the Harbour Inn."

She nodded. "Jesse seems nice," she said slyly.

Abandoning my downplaying I blurted out in a rush, "Yes Grandma, he seems really nice! He's funny and smart and athletic and likes camping and canoeing and should be able to get a really good job when he's done his program and he's thinking of trying to get on at Douglas Point and live up here when he graduates." I paused for a breath.

She nodded and said, "Not bad to look at either."

"Grandma!" I admonished, laughing.

"Hey," she said, "I may be old, but I'm not dead."

Chapter Ten

A few days later, we were waiting for Grandpa's cousin, Martha, to arrive with Great Grandma's diaries, and I dithered around as if Leonardo DeCaprio was coming for lunch.

Poor Grandma was peppered with questions about the diaries. "Do you think they're from when Grandpa was growing up? Do you think she wrote some when she lived in England? Wouldn't it be interesting if she wrote about her voyage to Canada?" Of course Grandma didn't know any more about the diaries than I, so she just laughed and shook her head at my ill-contained excitement.

Great Aunt Martha was a few years younger than Grandma and Grandpa. She walked with a sure step, had dark grey wavy hair and black rimmed glasses, and wore a lavender dress with matching earrings. After hugs and hellos on the deck, Martha handed me a shoe box to carry into the house. While walking behind the two older ladies, I slipped off the lid and saw a pile of old blue scribblers. Laying my hand on top of the pile, it actually felt like some kind of energy radiated up from the scribblers and I snatched back my hand as if it were burnt. I shook my head and silently scolded myself. Sometimes my imagination could get out of hand.

Lunch was delicious but took way too long. I scurried about and cleared first course, warmed up Grandma's raisin pie, and made tea. But despite my best efforts to move things along, the older people, for some reason, were not in a hurry to finish the meal. It felt rude to leave the table to start reading the diaries, but I did finger the scribblers, and before they finished their first of three (count them, three) cups of tea, I had the diaries arranged in chronological order.

The first entry was dated July 15, 1910, which by my calculations was a couple months before Great Grandma Sadie's fifteenth birthday, meaning she was still in England. The last entry was written on February 21, 1925. A quick glance revealed that Sadie was quite agitated, saying she was afraid Cecil would find her diaries, and if he did she knew he would burn them and "*I don't know what else he might do.*" She was worried there wasn't a safe place to hide them. So, maybe she ended up giving them to her sister to hide? When I shared this idea with the group, they agreed it was very possible.

Martha indicated that her own mother, Agnes, immigrated to Canada in April 1925, about three months after Sadie's last diary entry, so Sadie could have given the diaries to her. And over the next fifty odd years Great Grandma Sadie never got the diaries back... how very sad.

As soon as Martha left, Grandma turned to me and laughed. "I thought you were going to burst if you had to wait another minute to get reading those diaries! Go ahead. They should be read in order. You take the first one, share the highlights with us, and then later I'll read them myself."

I grinned. "Thanks Grandma," I said. "I'll go down to the pond lawn." Then I charged out the door with the box of diaries.

Parking myself on a lawn chair, I reverently opened the first small scribbler, which was dated July 15, 1910. Great Aunt Sadie would have been 15. In small, precise handwriting, Sadie had written, *"Today I started my apprentice at A. & W. Flatau Shoe Manufacturers."*

Chapter Eleven

London, England | 1910

Although it was kind of scary, Sadie was excited about her new job. Her best friends from school, Maisy and Emma, started at the factory on the same day, and they met at the tram stop on Wilson Road at six-fifteen in the morning. From half a block away, Sadie saw Maisy waving at her and jumping up and down with excitement. Sadie smiled and shook her head fondly at her exuberant friend. As she walked closer she realized that Maisy was already chattering at her.

"…and after that silly dream I never did get back to sleep, so I've been awake since four!" Maisy was a lively girl. Her body was short and plump, her red hair short and bouncy, and she had a bubbly personality.

Sadie laughed and bent down to give Maisy a hug. Sadie's long chestnut hair was neatly rolled, but after the exuberance of her friend's hug, it needed some attention. Emma joined them as Sadie re-inserted three hair pins. Emma was tall and slim like Sadie, and had her black hair pulled up into a roll as well.

Sadie smiled and raised up her brows over intense green eyes while nodding in Maisy's direction. "Watch out for your hairdo," she said. The three girls giggled.

Maisy grabbed her friends' hands. "Can you believe we're really starting work today? No more school… it might be just as boring, but at least we'll get paid!" They laughed as the tram pulled up, then they paid their fare, and clamoured up the curving steps to the second level.

Sadie, always practical, said, "We get off at Downhill Street and walk another three blocks, almost to St. Thomas' Road. The owners of the shoe factory are brothers, Albert and Willard Flatau."

A few minutes later they approached the factory, an austere red brick building with grimy windows along all sides. They were soon joined by a few other girls, and a supervisor gave them a quick tour through the three floors of the building. The noise was overwhelming and although the man yelled out the name of each type of machine, Sadie felt dazed and couldn't make out half of what he said. The biggest machines were operated by men, but women used many of the smaller ones, and Sadie swallowed hard at the thought of working with one of the strange contraptions.

Eventually, the new workers were herded into a separate room and the door was closed, which lessened the noise only slightly. They were each given a heavy iron shoe anvil and a little hammer, which was more like a short iron rod, blunt on one end and slightly pointed on the other. They had to fit a partially completed shoe over the anvil and tack on the sole, but only hammering in the tacks half-way, so that later they could be removed after the pieces were properly attached by machine. The girls were also given some finished products so they could practice removing the holding tacks.

At one o'clock, all the machines on the floor shut down. It was lunch time. Most people stayed at their stations to eat or moved around to be near friends.

Maisy pointed to a few people leaving the building and said, "Look, we can have lunch outside."

They grabbed their lunch pails and headed down the dusty stairs and out the main door. They found a couple of rocks to sit on, and Sadie hungrily dug into a thick slice of bread and a chunk of cheese.

The girls chattered excitedly, but after just a few minutes an older woman came over to them with a caution. "If you have to use the loo, you better get into the line-up. You'll catch it from the bosses if our thirty minutes is up and you're not back at your stations."

Sadie drained the last of the cold tea in her mason jar, and the three friends scurried off to find the loo line-up, still munching on their lunch.

That afternoon, all the new girls were placed in the line. Maisy and Sadie were pleased that they were both on the third floor and pretty close to each other, but poor Emma was taken downstairs to the first floor, which meant she would have a different lunch break than her friends.

Sadie was nervous and flustered by the din and ruckus of machines on both sides of her, and while putting the third "upper" over the form, she dropped her little hammer, which rolled under the big machine behind her. The machine had to be turned off while Sadie went down on her hands and knees in the choking dust to retrieve it. The man operating the machine shot some nasty words her way, the supervisor glared at her, and Sadie was close to tears as she returned to her spot. She glanced towards Maisy two rows over, who quickly averted her eyes and pressed her lips hard together, apparently swallowing a snicker.

Gradually Sadie became quicker and more confident at her task. The afternoon seemed to go on forever, but the five o'clock whistle finally blew, and the machines ground to a halt. Sadie and Maisy jostled with the crowd down two flights of stairs and out the main door, where they managed to find Emma.

They headed to the tram stop and once on board, Maisy started relating the story of Sadie dropping her hammer. "The bloke behind you had steam coming out of his ears. He looked like he was about to explode! Oh Sara, your face went even whiter that usual. Your freckles looked about to jump off your face! And the supervisor frowned so hard and shook his head." Maisy imitated both motions. "It was as if you'd started the place on fire or something!"

Sadie and Emma gasped with laughter, while at the same time tried to shush Maisy for fear of other factory workers overhearing.

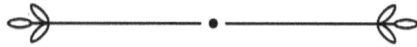

Sadie's first day at the factory was monumental for a second reason. Not only had she started her new job, but she had also summoned up the courage to walk away from her father's nightly Bible readings. For as long as she could remember, she and her younger sister Agnes were forced to sit at the kitchen table for two hours every evening, listening to their father read Bible passages out loud. Resting beside the Bible on the table was the "scripture stick," as the girls privately called it. If either sister nodded off or looked inattentive, they received a quick whack on the head or knuckles with the stick. The whole affair was deadly boring and Sadie had decided a month ago to use her new job as an excuse to break away from the evening drudgery.

Immediately after the supper dishes were cleaned and put away, Sadie summoned up her courage, "Father, I'm so sorry, but because of my new position, I'll have to excuse myself from the evening Bible studies." Before her stunned Father could respond, she continued. "I'm just so exhausted and I don't want to be injured or lose my job because I can't stay awake."

She started walking towards the stairway and continued to apologize, briefly meeting her sister's dagger eyes on the way. She quickly rushed upstairs, and to her complete surprise and delight, her father did not bellow for her to return.

Sadie stood listening at the door of the bedroom she shared with her sister until her father's droning Bible voice started up. Then she quietly closed the door, dashed to her bed, and collapsed face-down, laughing into her pillow. It was unbelievable that her plot had worked! She briefly hoped God would not strike her dead on the spot, and knew there'd be bloody hell to pay from her sister, but she didn't care. She was free of the evening torture. After changing into her night clothes, Sadie laid on her bed and had just enough light from the gas street lamp outside her window to write in her new diary and to read a few pages of *Jane Eyre*, nodding off with the book laying open on her chest.

At one o'clock the following Saturday, Sadie and her friends finished their exhausting week of work and received their very first pay.

Maisy was giddy with excitement. "We have to stop at a flower cart and buy posies. There's one on the corner of Mullberry."

So began a tradition. Every Saturday after work, the girls each purchased a posy of purple violets to pin onto the shoulder of their dresses. That first payday, the friends had big plans.

"I'm so glad we're staying at your place tonight," Sadie said to Emma. "That way my father can't interfere with our evening. He's getting more and more austere and peculiar."

Months earlier, while still at school, the girls had decided that with their first pay, they would go to the brand new Electric Cinema on Portobello Road in Notting Hill. It was one of only two theatres in London that were built specifically for the new moving pictures, and the girls were going to see *Henry the Eighth*.

The three friends were wildly excited and arrived at the theatre a full hour before show time. They had often admired the terra cotta brick of the cinema, with the galvanized zinc archway and the stunning zinc dome, but they had never been inside. Proudly, they handed over four pence each at the box office booth, and then, holding hands and their breath, they reverently stepped inside.

The high ceiling and the white pillars reminded them of a church, but at the far end of the lobby was an ornate golden archway inlaid with a huge map of the world. "It's like we're being invited to see the world through the eyes of the moving pictures," Maisy whispered.

All three girls giggled with delight as they were each handed an orange and a sweet bun to take to their balcony seats. When the orchestra started playing, they held hands in excitement, and when the dialogue or plot notes appeared on the screen, they quietly whispered them in unison.

An hour later, while walking back to Emma's flat, they chattered excitedly. "The costumes were amazing, all those beads and jewelry, and layers and layers of fabric," said Emma.

"And old Henry in his stockings and dress!" added Maisy, and they all giggled.

"I still can hardly believe that we watched actors who were not actually present in the room. Amazing," mused Emma.

"I just loved the music," exclaimed Sadie. "So dramatic, so inspiring, so many different instruments. It was breathtaking."

The evening was a fantasy come true and they were smitten. From then on, Sadie and her two friends went to see a moving picture show every second Saturday night.

After a few months at the factory, Sadie started training on the Hand Method Folding Machine. "It's so loud," she told her sister, Agnes, "and a bit daunting." But Sadie made good progress, and within a month was as fast as the other women on the Folding Machines.

After several weeks on the machine, Sadie mentioned to Maisy and Emma as they travelled home on the tram, "It's curious, but on our way home lately my ears have a peculiar feeling of fullness. And sometimes I hear some odd ringing in them." However, since both these issues usually disappeared by the time she arrived home, Sadie was not particularly concerned.

To her immense relief, Sadie's father never challenged her decision to forego the evening Bible sessions; however, over the next few months, Agnes often complained to her sister.

"The readings are getting worse and worse. More often than not, he chooses passages about punishment, plagues, and murder," she sighed. "It's quite dismal."

The girls' father had also started repeating Bible verses from memory during the family's walk to church and back each Sunday.

"Sorry, Agnes," Sadie whispered to her sister. "I assume these extra lessons are directed at me, to make up for the missed after-dinner preaching."

"I suppose so," her sister sighed. "He's become so tiresome. I can't wait until I start work and can skip the evening penance like you do. Just not sure how I can tolerate it for another year and a half."

Chapter Twelve

*I*t was the first of June and mother nature had gifted us an outstanding day to start the new month. It held promises of hot summer days, long summer evenings, and fresh beginnings. I felt full of energy and decided to attack the job of painting the little cabin down by the pond.

Meanwhile, Grandma had decided to tackle the lawns and was outfitted in a large floppy sun hat and an old, long-sleeved white shirt of Grandpa's. I walked beside her as she drove her scooter down to the shed. Grandpa had gassed and oiled the riding lawn mower, and he stood beside it, shaking his head at Grandma.

"You're really going to do this, are you?" he asked her.

She bristled. "Well, I just have to sit there," she said. "And you know I've always liked mowing the lawns." She got off the scooter and shuffled to the mower. We both helped her climb aboard.

"You remember how to start it?" Grandpa asked (*foolishly*, I thought to myself).

Grandma gave him a stony look, narrowed her eyes, and said, "Of course I remember how to start it. I expect I've spent more time on this mower than you have."

"I expect you're right about that," he agreed. "But could I just ask one thing of you? I'd be forever grateful if you did not mow around the pond. Let me do that. I don't want you driving off the dam and ending up in the drink."

"Why? It's better if you end up in the drink?" she sniffed.

"I won't end up in the drink; but yes, if one of us did, I would rather it was me." He shook his head again and smiled. "Just let me do the damn dam, woman."

Grandma huffed but said, "Fine, I won't do the damn dam."

"Thank you. And if you have any trouble, just turn off the mower and I'll come to you. I'm going to feed the cattle. Sara, will you listen for the mower stopping and come get me if needed?"

Having had trouble keeping a straight face during the previous exchange, I only trusted myself to say, "Yep," and clamped my lips together.

Grandma roared the mower into life, threw Grandpa a smug look, and headed out towards the front lawn. Walking directly behind her and the mower allowed me to laugh out loud without either one hearing. (I hoped).

For the next two days, I scraped flaking paint from the exterior walls and trim of the cabin, all while relishing the sunshine, the heat, and the heady aroma of lilacs and freshly cut lawns. It took two more days to give all the trim a double coat of paint. Late on Friday afternoon, when I was painting the first wall, Uncle Scott stopped at the cabin on his way back from the fields. He left the truck running and the door open, and while he walked towards me, whipped off his Horizon Seed cap and mopped his damp forehead with the bottom of his t-shirt.

"Sara," he said, as he got close, "we're going to be haying tomorrow. It depends how heavy the dew is, but hopefully the first load will be baled by ten."

"Okay, I'll be ready."

This change of duties pleased me. It seemed the cabin and I had been spending a bit too much time together, and we needed a break. Also, I knew from previous experience that the after haying swim was the champion of all swims.

Sure enough, by ten o'clock the next morning I was slugging bales. Most farmers produced huge round or square bales that were moved about with a fork on the front of a tractor. However, later in the season, Scott sold old-fashioned small bales to the horse raceways down-country, and since the fields at Grandma and Grandpa's were too small for the bigger machinery anyway, the hay here was baled and man/woman-handled in the old fashioned manner. I was on the wagon putting bales on the elevator (which is really more like an escalator), and Jesse was stacking the bales in the high mow. I had the easier job, as Jess had to carry the bales further, plus it would be hotter in the mow. In between loads, Jesse took the empty wagon to the back of the farm and retrieved a full one from Scott, who was driving the tractor with the baler attached. This was usually Grandpa's job, but he was away at an appointment. By 11:45 Jesse arrived back at the barn with the third wagon load.

"Scott says after this load, it's swim time," he told me. "He'll bring the next load up when he comes for lunch." To my considerable dismay, Jesse confessed he had never gone swimming right after slugging bales.

"I'm certain you will never feel the same about a regular run-of-the-mill swim," I told him.

When we arrived at the edge of the pond, he immediately ran in full speed, swam half-way across, and then whooped, "Outstanding!"

Meanwhile, I inched in slowly, but eventually caught up to him. We both swam to the far side and half-way back, after which we floated on our backs and took turns talking while the other one had his or her ears under water. This was followed by "What did you say?" Pause, repeat, and then we started the sequence all over again.

That afternoon, we took off three more loads and then had pizza for supper, which Grandpa had picked up in town. After supper, we unloaded the final two wagons of the day, but this time Scott and Stacy helped, and we were well supervised by Brandon, Molly, Grandma, and Grandpa. As the last bale moved up the elevator, there was a cheer from all, and then the entire group headed to the pond. Following my third and final swim of the day, I barely made it up the two flights of stairs to crash onto my bed.

The next day was Sunday. Unless the crops and weather had been desperately at odds with each other for some time, Scott did not work on Sundays. Well, except for the two hours morning and night of milking and feeding eighty cows.

Since it looked like we'd be back at the hay on Monday, I decided to finish painting the cabin. At the mid-afternoon home stretch—with earbuds in and doing a salsa/rollering type dance while I bellowed out the lyrics of "Smooth" along with Santana and Rob Tomlinson—I caught a movement out of the corner of my eye. Jesse was standing a few feet away in his bathing suit, towel over his shoulder, laughing his head off. I took off after him with the roller, but by the time we got halfway across the pond lawn, it was clear he could outrun me.

"Okay, I'll forgive you for sneaking up on me if you get me a beer from the fridge in the cabin," I panted. "And if you quit laughing, you can have one too."

So Jesse kept me company while I finished the last wall. Then we went for a swim, topped off with another beer while stretched out on the lawn. He inquired about my teacher's program and seemed quite interested that I had recently applied to local school boards. He asked about other family in the area, and I told him about Uncle Ray, describing a bit of his history and his current living situation.

"A couple weeks ago, I went with Grandma and Grandpa to take Ray out to lunch, but it was so awkward and stilted. He hardly talked and rarely responded to anything we said. The poor guy, I really should try to see him more often, but it's so challenging."

To my astonishment, Jesse said, "I'll go visit him with you sometime. If you want. Maybe we can think of something he might enjoy doing."

"That would be amazing," I said.

We both gazed across the water for a few minutes, until he asked, "Does the pond have any fish in it?"

"Yep, Grandpa stocks it with trout. I caught a good sized one last year but haven't been fishing yet this year."

"Oh, cool. So we should go fishing. And maybe sometime we can go down to the river. I'm sure Scott would let us borrow the truck to take the canoe down, if that was okay."

I liked the sound of those ideas. Yes, Jesse seemed to be getting more interesting all the time.

On Monday, we finished haying at noon and got in another swim before lunch. By five, the sky had darkened with hammerheads of clouds looming high in the north, and mutterings of thunder in the air. The rain started around six, but the thunder and lightening remained aloof, close enough to notice but not close enough to shatter your nerves.

Chapter Thirteen

There were two days of rain, and then Scott and Jesse spent five days cutting, raking, and waiting for more hay to dry enough to bale. The following Monday we were at it again, with Grandpa running the empty wagons to the field and bringing back the full ones. As we waited between loads, Jesse and I sat just inside the barn, near the big open doorway, enjoying the sweet, baked smell of fresh hay and an occasional half-hearted puff of breeze. We chugged some water, stretched out on the loose hay beneath us, and gazed at the high vertical lines of sunlight gleaming through the end boards of the barn.

"This barn is amazing," Jesse said. Flabbergasted that he was interested in the old building, I launched into a recital of all my bank-barn knowledge, honed from Grandpa and Google.

"Last summer, Grandpa and I measured the barn and it's sixty feet long, forty feet wide, and about forty feet high at the peak, which means those two beams"—and I pointed to the beams running from one end of the barn to the other—"are sixty feet long, each made from a single tree! I can't imagine how they transported them here, a hundred years ago, let alone hauled them up there and made them stay put. Grandpa said they'd have used a pulley powered by teams of horses. And all the beams were hand-squared with an axe... you can see the chopping marks on them, especially those big beams going across the width," I said, pointing. "Those beauties are twelve inches square."

"They're massive," Jesse said. "Just imagine how heavy they must be, and how did they find such straight trees? Look," he said, pointing. "They're held together with wooden pegs." He was impressed. "Do you know when it was built?"

"Well, Grandma and Grandpa think probably in the 1880s because they know its older than the house which was built around 1898."

Jesse whistled appreciatively.

Pointing to the peak of the roof, I said, "You can see part of the old pulley hoist up there. Apparently, when mom was a kid, a big rope still hung from that, and my uncle and his cousin would climb up to one of those huge beams and swing on the rope over to the beam on the other side, often with machinery sitting on the floor here underneath."

"Wow," said Jesse. "That's crazy. What was the rope for?"

"It would have had a big clamp on it to hoist up loose hay or straw into the mow, before farmers had balers. Anyway, when Grandpa found out about the swing game, he took the rope down." Then, feeling a little smug, I asked Jess, "Do you know why it's called a bank barn?" I was practically bursting to tell him.

But to my dismay, he said, "Well, I guess because it's built into a bank."

Hiding my disappointment that he figured it out so easily, I confirmed, "Yep, you're right. It's so the animals can be on the first floor, but you can run machinery in up here. Plus, the hay and straw help keep the downstairs warmer in the winter. I used to think the term referred to an old-style money bank and had something to do with a vaulted ceiling. Smarty pants!" Rolling over, I gave him a punch in the arm.

He was indignant. "Hey, have some respect. You know I'm a gift, don't you? A gift from God. So show some appreciation!"

"Oh, I'll appreciate you getting me a cold beer after the last load!" I laughed. "What do you mean, you're a gift from God?"

"The name Jesse means gift… I may have embellished a bit about the God part. Do you know what the name Sara means?"

I did not, so he quickly consulted Google on his phone and after a couple minutes said, "Oh, oh," and moved to put his phone back in his pocket.

As I tried to grab it from him, he said. "No, no, this was a bad idea. "You'll be unbearable. I think there's something wrong with my phone." He gave it a shake, as if that would do anything. After some badgering from me, he finally said, "Well, it must be a mistake, but it says here that the name Sara means princess."

My eyes opened wide and I stared at him with abundant alarm.

"What?" he asked, "I thought you'd be all over this, making me bow to you and help you onto the hay wagon and stuff. What's going on?"

I tried to smile but it felt like more of a grimace. With a hollow laugh I mumbled something about him laying his shirt down for me to walk across the barnyard, but he wasn't amused. He looked at me quizzically, and then thankfully we heard the tractor rounding the end of the barn and hauled ourselves onto our feet for the next load.

Late that afternoon, after a well-earned swim, Jesse and I sat on the pond lawn, each with a half-empty beer can in hand. He flopped onto his back, with one arm underneath his head and said, "Running rabbit, twelve o'clock."

Looking at him, I briefly scrunched up my face into a "what?" expression before I caught on, laughed, and laid back too. "Oh, good one," I said, then after a brief pause, "monster cookie-monster straight up."

"Right!" he said. "I can't believe I didn't see that first."

The random clouds were perfect for shape-spotting and we quickly managed to come up with a crocodile hauling himself over a fluffy bank, a sheep (of course), and I found a perfectly shaped Flounder, the scrappy fish from *The Little Mermaid*. I was shocked when Jesse told me he had never seen *The Little Mermaid*.

"Oh, it's my favourite Disney movie. And it's not as girlie as you might think... it has sea monsters, great music, and is really funny and cute."

"I dunno," he said. "Cute sounds kind of girlie to me."

After I elbowed him in response, we sat up to sip our beer. I kept my eyes on the barn swallows methodically swooping over the pond. The silence between us could only last so long, and I braced myself.

"So what was that deal with your name all about?" he asked.

After fiddling with the label on my beer, then pulling some bits of grass from the lawn, I finally looked out across the water and took a big breath. "Okay," I said. "So I'm going to tell you some stuff, and you should know that it gets pretty bizarre, and you may conclude that I'm crazy, which very well could be the case. Just remember, you asked."

I told him everything. I told him about the coffin nightmare and about the little girl dream, and that she always said my name three times. I told him about Raving Rasputin and that my sister had verified his Bible quotes. I told him about crazy Great Great Aunt Agnes who also called my name; about Uncle Ray and the "too many children" connection. I told him that I had seen the girl in the daytime too... still saying my name three times.

Finally, taking a big breath, I added the last piece. "So, along with the Bible references, Rasputin often babbles about 'my princess'... so when you told me that Sara means princess..."

As I studied his face, his eyebrows shot up and he let out a whistle. "Wow," he said, "I can see why the princess thing freaked you out."

"It just gets weirder and weirder, Jesse. And I don't know what it all means, or how to make it all stop."

I thought he might run for the hills (or just tell me he had to go home). But instead he asked, "Have you written all this down? We need to work on this like detectives, look for clues, research possibilities. There are probably connections and questions that will be more obvious if all the details are written down and we can study them. We can figure this out. I'm sure we can."

But all I really heard was "we." He wasn't running for the hills, and suddenly, to my complete surprise, there were tears trickling down my cheeks. Covering my face with my hands I whispered, "I'm sorry for being so sappy, but I just can't believe you said we... *we* can figure this out."

For the first time ever, he put his arms around me. He

pulled me towards him and I sniffled into his bare chest.

"Hey, did you think I was going to run for the hills or something?" he asked. I nodded my head, smearing a wet cheek against his bare chest, and we both laughed.

Jesse's arms around me felt comfortable and right. Eventually, he rubbed my arm a bit and asked, "Do you have all those Bible quotes that your sister figured out on your laptop?" I nodded. "So why don't we build our research around that document?" he said.

"Okay," I responded and there was silence for a couple minutes.

"So… do you want to go and get your laptop?" he asked.

"You mean right now?"

"Well, why not?"

So I headed to the house, brought out my laptop, and opened the Bible quote file. We agreed I would dictate while Jesse entered the information and organized the file. We were at it for an hour and a half, with Jesse quizzing me for as many details as possible.

Just when I thought we were done, he said, "Wait, what about the crazy lady who goes out the window and around the house?"

"But I don't know if she has anything to do with anything."

"She calls your name, doesn't she? It could be related. I'm going to include her." And he did.

Later that evening, walking around the pond by myself, I pondered something that hadn't been shared with

Jesse. Sometimes, early in the morning I wake with the little girl on my mind, and it feels like we have just been together, in a natural, non-weird kind of way. But during the transition from dream-state to wakefulness, the memory fractures. Her presence dances at the edges of my mind, but she slips away from me. It's like trying to catch smoke from a campfire; it's right there, but if you try to grasp it, it swirls out of your reach. It feels like something important has been lost… something I'm supposed to know.

Chapter Fourteen

On the following Saturday morning, Grandma and Grandpa picked up Uncle Ray and brought him to the farm for an overnight visit. I made chilli while pondering a way to cultivate a relationship with Ray, a way to make a little fracture in his rigid shell. During lunch, Grandma and I chatted about gardening and family, but Uncle Ray remained stoically unresponsive.

Eventually, Grandma mentioned that Stacy would be dropping off Buzz on Sunday morning, and this was the information that finally elicited a reaction. Ray actually looked toward Grandma and said, "Good." Ray loved that dog. Well, I guess he loved dogs in general, but when he was with Buzz, he was the happiest we ever see him.

Sometimes, when Scott has to go to Owen Sound, he takes Buzz along and picks up Ray to go for a walk together.

After lunch, Uncle Ray immediately took his overnight bag up to his room on the second floor. He was an avid reader and often sat up there for hours engrossed in a book; but by late afternoon, Grandma was fussed about him being "squirrelled away" and asked if I could try to convince him to come down.

I wandered upstairs and was relieved to find his door ajar. He was sitting at the small desk in front of the window with his back to the door, hunched over a book lying flat in front of him. When I tapped on the door, he lifted his head but did not turn to face me.

"Uncle Ray, it's really nice outside, I was wondering if you might like to walk to the back of the farm with me?"

Ray continued to stare out the window, but after a pause he surprised me by saying, "Okay."

"Great," I said. "So we should go pretty soon because supper time is not too far away."

Ray nodded, pushed back his chair, and silently followed me down the stairs. When we got to the entrance way, he continued to the big room and pulled binoculars out of the sideboard drawer. I told Grandma and Grandpa we were going for a walk and in unison like grey-topped bobble heads, they nodded approvingly.

When we got to the other side of the barn, Uncle Ray spotted a large bird at the top of a tree halfway down the first field. He stopped and looked through the binoculars, tracking the bird as it took off and glided effortlessly out of sight.

Deciding to take a chance I asked, "What kind of bird was it?"

"Red tailed hawk," he said with no hesitation, and started walking again. Partway back the lane we were severely scolded by a chubby black squirrel on a nearby post who flicked his tail in a meaningful manner. Reaching the back field, I asked Ray if we should take the trail through the pine bush, and he nodded, so we headed south across a mixture of hay stubble and fresh green growth already sprouting up—the beginnings of the second crop of hay.

Partway across the field, Ray suddenly put his hand on my upper arm to stop me. I looked at him in surprise, then followed his gaze. A deer had emerged from the hardwood bush to the north and stopped a few feet into the field. It glanced our way, then looked back into the bush as two more deer leapt from the trees. In single file, they bounded east with a fluid, easy grace that was breathtaking. It seemed as though they actually flowed across the field, like a brook flows over rocks.

"So beautiful," I whispered, and Ray nodded.

We continued towards the pine bush, and walked the trail with majestic pines towering above us. Searching for a conversation topic, I asked, "How tall would these trees be?"

Ray glanced skyward and said, "Forty to forty-five feet."

"And how old would they be?"

"Planted when you were a toddler, so about twenty-one to twenty-two years, I guess."

It was surprising that Ray remembered this and also that he knew my age. My mom had photos of me on her lap and Beth beside her, all sitting on the stone-bolt with shovels and hoes beside us, and Grandma at the wheel of the little Ford tractor, hauling us across a field. There was also a photo of me playing in the dirt, while 4-year-old Beth carefully nestled a twelve-inch tree into a hole, with Grandpa leaning on a shovel, supervising.

The two of us walked to the far end of the pines and then followed the path single-file through an area of scrub bushes and tall grasses. Part-way around I realized Ray was no longer with me, and back-tracked to find him studying a flattened-down area off to the side of the path. With hands on hips, I looked at the flat grass then turned my gaze questioningly to Uncle Ray.

"Deer yard," he said succinctly, without looking at me. In my ongoing efforts to encourage conversation, I queried the term and was pleased when he responded. "Deer will lay down there all together, especially in the winter, but clearly they're still using it now."

Wow, a complete sentence. Impressive.

Back at the house I headed upstairs, but on the way through the kitchen, suggested that Grandma encourage Ray to recount what we saw on our walk. Upon returning downstairs after my shower, Grandma secretively gave me a thumbs-up, and I felt rewarded for my efforts of making a connection, however small, with Uncle Ray.

At ten o'clock the next morning, Stacy arrived from down the road with their dog. Buzz exploded out of her car and was barking at the farmhouse door before she had the car hatch closed. I let Buzz in and he greeted me with wild enthusiasm, then launched himself towards the big room and Ray, who actually smiled as the whirlwind practically wagged his tail off and covered him with adoring licks. He took a quick break to acknowledge Grandma and Grandpa, then dashed back to Ray's side.

Grandpa laughed and said, "Buzz, should we take you out for a game of stick?" At the word "stick," Buzz hurtled himself back towards the door, with me quickly sidestepping out of his way, and Ray and Grandpa shuffling after him. They threw a stick for that dog for an hour, sometimes into the pond and sometimes on the lawns, until finally Buzz actually laid down and grinned up at them with his tongue cascaded down to the grass.

Ray spent the entire day outside with the dog. After lunch, he decided to take Buzz for a walk back to the end of the lane, and Grandma and Grandpa toured alongside them in the golf cart. With the dog by his side, Ray's whole body language completely changed. The tenseness left his face, a sparkle was in his eyes, and his step was lighter.

Immediately after supper, Ray, Buzz, and I headed out to my car. Buzz squeezed in at Ray's feet—well, his front half was actually on Ray's lap. As we approached Stacy and Scott's place, the dog started squealing and yipping in excitement, and when the car stopped and Ray opened the door, Buzz exited the vehicle like he'd been shot from a cannon. The kids were on the side lawn and he stormed over and greeted them as though they had been separated for months and he had suffered from a complete lack of social interaction since they were last together. His attack was met with squeals of delight from the kids, and a loud chase game immediately ensued.

Looking over at Ray, I saw him stiffen slightly and close his window against the shrieks. He stared straight ahead, pointedly not watching the wild antics outside. His face closed in again, and his hands resting on his thighs were tightly clenched.

Jesse wandered out of the house and climbed into the back seat. The two of us were going to a movie in Owen Sound, and we were taking Ray back to the group home en route. Wondering if Ray was offended about Buzz being so excited to see the kids, I said to Jesse, "That dog was just as wildly excited to come to our place and see Ray. He is a perpetual cyclone!"

"Yep, he's a whirling bundle of joyfulness." Jesse laughed. "He can be exhausting to live with, but you have to admire his zeal for life!"

When we got to the group home, I said, "We'll see you soon, Uncle Ray. I enjoyed your visit, especially our walk. Seeing those deer was amazing."

Ray did not respond, but got out of the car, collected his bag from the back seat, walked up the porch steps, and disappeared inside the house.

Jesse moved to the front seat of the car. "Chatty fellow, isn't he?"

Shaking my head, I told him about our walk and also how Ray's whole demeanour had changed so completely with the dog. "Then the noise of the kids clammed him right back up again."

"Too bad he couldn't have his own dog at the group home," Jess said.

"Yes, we all think so. About a year ago, Grandma and Grandpa tried to convince the group home director of that, but had no success."

We made our way to the movie theatre at the other end of town and saw *The Bourne Supremacy,* which included enough car-chase scenes to satisfy Jesse, and enough shirtless Matt Damon scenes to satisfy me.

Chapter Fifteen

*M*onday was grey and overcast and I decided to spend most of the day reading Great Grandma Sadie's diaries, so after breakfast I installed myself in the porch with the scribblers and a cup of tea. Outside, the sun shone briefly through a small gap in the clouds, but most of the sky was rippled with dullness.

London, England | 1911-1912

Sadie's diary entries throughout the first half of 1911 focused mainly on her continued work at the factory, as well as outings with her girlfriends to the Electric Cinema, to football games, and a couple times to the London Zoo. She documented Maisy and Emmas' rotating crushes on local boys, but Sadie never elaborated about any love interests of her own.

On a lovely Sunday afternoon in May, Sadie, and her sister Agnes went for a walk along the river. The conversation turned to their father, who had started randomly quoting Bible verses at any time or place throughout the day.

"Father has become so tiresome with his constant preaching and his gloomy outlook on life," complained Agnes. "And he's so incredibly irritated all the time. I can't do anything right around him. He makes me so nervous that, sure enough, I'll break a dish or something, and that will set him off on a tirade for an hour."

"I know. It's impossible to please him or to have any kind of conversation with him. He's become truly obsessed with the Bible. I don't know what we can do."

During July, August, and September of 1911, the city of London was shrouded in an overwhelming heat wave and early in the summer, *The Times* began a regular column titled *Deaths from Heat.* Many factories including A. & W. Flatau, changed the working hours to avoid the oppressive heat of the afternoon. Trams started running all night, as workers came and went at odd hours. Sadie, Emma, and Maisy met at three in the morning on Victoria Road in order to be at work by four, and their shift was temporarily shortened from ten hours a day to eight, meaning they were finished at noon.

"I'm glad they took all the windows out in the factory, and thank goodness they have that boy going around with the water bucket and dipper all day," said Sadie.

"Even so, the air is stifling by seven o'clock and I feel positively limp from the heat after two hours on the line," complained Maisy.

Back at home, Sadie and Agnes dragged their sleeping pads to the backyard and used poles and old sheets to provide some daytime shade, but sleep was fitful and short.

As they lay awake one sweltering evening, Agnes said, "Between the heat and the lack of sleep, I think Father is about to explode."

Sadie shook her head. "I know. That eerie look he gets in his eyes frightens me."

"And the way he relates every tragic news story to a Bible passage... sometimes I just feel like screaming."

"Well, don't do it," cautioned her sister. "I think he could turn violent in a heartbeat."

Sadie's father wasn't the only one on the edge of violence; the entire city smouldered with anger and turmoil in the overwhelming heat. Riots and strikes were on-going occurrences as the work force became more and more dissatisfied with low wages, long hours, and unsafe working conditions. Some workers were laid off due to water shortages, and beyond the city in the scorched countryside, farmers struggled to provide feed and water to their animals.

At last, by the end of September, the heat wave dissipated, the temperatures cooled, and factory hours returned to the normal shifts. But strikes and unrest continued.

At 16 years of age, Sadie became interested in the

Suffragette movement but was appalled by some of their activities. "They think smashing shop windows proves they're intelligent enough and responsible enough to vote?" she lamented to her friends. "Bloody fools! How does acting like hoodlums help the situation?"

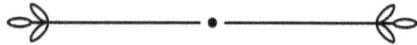

All the chaos and agitation on land was nothing compared to what happened at sea the following spring. On April 16, 1912, Sadie was almost to the tram stop in the morning, when Maisy bolted towards her, shouting and waving a newspaper, but Sadie could not make out her words. With a plummeting heart, she snatched the paper from her friend's hand and scanned the front page.

TITANIC SINKS read the headline, *Great Loss of Life; World's Greatest Liner Strikes Iceberg*. Unbelievably, it was reported that 1500 people had died on the maiden voyage of the "unsinkable" Titanic! When Sadie read that the band played music up to the last few minutes before the ship went under, tears ran down her face. Production in the factory decreased that day as dazed people tried to fathom the impossible.

By mid-May, the populace was desperate for summer to arrive and divert attention from the Titanic disaster. But summer of 1912 was not co-operative—with its cool temperatures and relentless rain, it turned out to be almost the exact opposite of the previous summer.

In late July, Emma voiced the feelings of everyone,

"Where is summer? I so need to feel some heat, and to see an actual blue sky, rather than this wretched, unending greyness and rain."

"It's horrible," Maisy agreed. "And of course the price of bread went up again."

Sadie shook her head. "The poor farmers; their crops are rotting in the field."

For two full days towards the end of August, solid sheets of rain pounded the southern half of Britain. People were killed, bridges were washed out, and in one area, floodwaters formed a lake a mile wide and twenty miles long. The Lee River on the eastern edge of Tottenham flooded streets and homes. The London Herald printed a photo of a lamp lighter in a row boat lighting the street lamps on flooded Towpath Road while three swans swam down the street in the background.

On the way to the factory, Sadie told Emma and Maisy, "Father has predictably interpreted the torrential rains and flooding as a Biblical sign. My decreased hearing is actually an advantage at home now, because I can't really make out most of his rants anymore."

Agnes, however, wanted to share the misery with her sister, so pointed out in the Bible, their father's uplifting message from Genesis 6:17. *"For behold, I will bring a flood of waters upon the earth to destroy all flesh in which is the breath of life under heaven. Everything that is on the earth shall die."*

The sisters avoided their father as much as possible.

In the spring of 1913, Sadie joined the National Union of Women's Suffrage Society (NUWSS). "The Society represents the law-abiding, non-militant women who believe in the vote for women," she explained to her mother and sister

The militant suffragettes however, escalated their violence, and acts of arson occurred at mail boxes, cricket pitches, and horse racing tracks. In February, the Tea House at Kew Gardens was set ablaze by suffragettes, and in June, Sadie came home with terrible news.

"At the Epsom Derby, Emily Davison ran out in front of the King's horse and was run over! They think she was trying to pin a "Votes for Women" banner on the horse. Oh, how could she be so reckless?" Four days later Emily Davison died of her injuries.

To provide hope and solidarity to its thousands of members, and to combat the violent reputation of the militant suffragettes, the NUWSS organized a nation-wide pilgrimage, which culminated on July 26, 1913 when 50,000 women gathered peacefully at Hyde Park in London. Proudly wearing their red, white, and green shoulder sashes, as well as the compulsory cockle shell badge pinned to their hats, Sadie and Agnes were part of the orderly crowd. It was exhilarating to participate in the movement for change, and the ensuing press reports were positive and promising.

The first half of 1914 was an exciting time; there was

change in the air. More and more motor-cars were on the streets and on three occasions Sadie had also seen a flying machine—or aeroplane—roar over the city. More stores and private homes had electricity, and the means to utilize that magical power seemed endless.

In May, Sadie wrote in her diary for the first time about a fellow named Walter.

'*I've been chumming around with Walter T. somewhat. Yesterday we went to the football game with the gang and he held my hand while we were walking. He wanted to take me to a film next weekend, with just the two of us, but I managed to turn it into another group outing. Not sure if he's happy about that! But I don't want to get serious... with him or anyone right now.*'

Sadie continued to be incensed with the militant suffragettes. One day in June, she arrived home and slammed a newspaper down on the table.

"I can't believe it! They've progressed to bombing churches, even Westminster Abbey! How could they? It's outrageous."

Sadie was also agitated by the German threats to peace and worried about rumours of war. In addition to everything else, she faced progressively more serious hearing problems. A doctor confirmed that her hearing was deficient, but did not offer any remedies or advice.

"At least I've become fairly proficient at reading people's lips," she told Maisy and Emma at lunch one day. "The thing I miss the most is hearing the music at *The Electric Cinema*. Thank goodness, with the written dialogue and explanations, I can understand the storyline as well as anyone."

On the morning of Wednesday August 5th, 1914, as Sadie walked to the tram, there was excitement and anticipation bristling in the air around her. Groups of people were talking and and waving newspapers. When Sadie met up with Maisy and Emma, she was full of questions, but Emma turned her towards a nearby paper boy and Sadie could read his lips as he bawled out, "Britain is at war! Asquith declares war on Germany!!"

Sadie's heart sank as she realized the monster she had been dreading was at the door. She fumbled in her bag for a penny to buy a copy of the Daily Express, and across the top of the front page in bold letters, it read *"England Expects That Every Man Will Do His Duty."* The first line underneath explained, *"Great Britain declared war on Germany at 11 o'clock last night."*

Sadie had difficulty maintaining her focus at work that day, but finally the whistle blew and the workers filed out. As the tram rattled along Downhill Street, Maisy and Emma decided to join a group of people heading towards the Central London Recruiting Depot, where apparently volunteers and reservists were swarming to sign up, and robust celebrations were occurring on the street.

Sadie was puzzled. "I don't understand this light-hearted eagerness about war."

"Oh, come on, Sadie," said Emma. "It's exciting. We should go down to the Depot. It will be like one big party."

But Sadie shook her head and frowned. "No, I'm not going to the Depot. This is not an event to celebrate."

"Sadie, you don't have to be so serious all the time," protested Maisy.

As Sadie rose to get off at her regular stop, she looked down into the eyes of her two friends and said, "War *is* serious."

Chapter Sixteen

Rural Ontario | 2005

At five-thirty, the porch door opened and Grandma poked her head out. "Will you be joining us inside for supper, Sara?"

Unbelievably, I'd been reading the diaries the entire day. If Grandma hadn't brought me a sandwich and a glass of milk at lunch time, I probably wouldn't have eaten at all. It felt like I'd been living and breathing Sadie's life in London almost a hundred years ago. As I stood, stretched, and registered my surroundings, it was apparent that the day was still on the edge of rain.

After dinner there was a brief shower—enough to knock the dust down, but not enough to help the thirsty fields.

A few days later, July arrived in the form of a simmering hot day with the humidity hanging thick and heavy in the air. I was intent on distracting myself from thinking about Raving Rasputin, who had invaded my sleep again the previous night. Somehow he seemed even scarier since Beth confirmed that his rants included real Bible quotes. Sitting on the shady deck with my laptop, I checked school board websites for new postings, while simultaneously catching up on friends' activities through Facebook. Grandma and Grandpa were hunkered down inside with the air conditioning.

It was the fourth day of a major heat wave and the crops and lawns were parched. A scattering of rain drops had splatted down earlier, but nothing useful developed. It may have just been the sky sweating. The flamboyant peonies in the perennial beds had burst forth by the dozens, but after a day in the sweltering heat, they hung their heads with exhaustion.

An hour later, the wind picked up and created a summer symphony through the swirling, dancing trees. Taking my laptop inside, I gave the octogenarians a weather update, and they decided to join me on the breezy deck for a while.

Grandma sat with her back to the wind, and her fine white curls flattened forwards. "After supper we're going down to Scone to play cards," she informed me.

"Last time we went, Red here won the big prize for the most lone hands," Grandpa added.

"Oh," I said. "What was the prize?"

Grandma laughed and shook her head at Grandpa, "A can of pork and beans."

"Had it the next day for lunch," he grinned. "It was a good can of free beans."

My heart swelled with love for these two people, the way they teased each other, depended on each other, and looked out for each other. They were coming up to their sixty-third wedding anniversary and had been a marriage role-model for decades.

Later, when the old people departed for Scone, I decided to walk back the lane. Lingering breezes tempered the humidity, but rain continued to elude us. A bunny zig-zagged ahead of me, paused, flicked his ears, and disappeared into the tall grasses along the old fence row. After walking to the edge of the hardwood bush, I turned back towards the farmhouse. The western sky was painted with a pale wash of pink and grey and I felt the day draw in on itself.

As the shades and shadows of evening arrived, I tried to avoid thinking about last night's dream, but the harder I tried, the tighter my chest felt, and the faster my heart beat. Blast.

An hour later, it was completely dark outside, and the empty house closed in on me. I turned on the TV and flicked channels, then pulled out my cell and phoned Jesse. "Hey, what's going on up there?" I asked. He responded that he had just come in from the barn and was about to have a shower.

"Grandma and Grandpa went to play cards and I can't get Rasputin out of my head. I had another nightmare about him last night."

Apparently I was pretty transparent, because Jesse immediately asked, "Hey, why don't I come down? I'll bring a couple movies."

Jesse arrived on the scene twenty minutes later with a package of microwaveable popcorn and two DVDs. I looked at the movies and laughed. He had brought *The Little Mermaid* and *Shrek*.

"Outstanding," he quipped, and I looked at him questioningly. "I was hoping to see that smile. But before we start a movie, you tell me about the nightmare, and let's get it all out of your head for tonight."

Taking a big breath, I nodded, and grabbed a couple beer from the fridge. Then we sat at the kitchen island.

"Okay," he said. "Give it up."

Jesse got the full story of the previous night's Raving Rasputin event, but when my account was finished, he didn't respond. I twirled my beer around while avoiding eye contact, but he was watching me.

After a bit, he said quietly, "What else?"

Sighing, I gazed out the dark window while tapping a fingernail on the counter at a manic speed. Jesse waited quietly as I progressed to ripping the label from the beer bottle. He took a sip of his beer and said nothing.

Tidying the bits into a little pile on the counter top, I finally blurted out, "But what I keep thinking about… what I'm really afraid of… is that Rasputin will appear in the daytime like the little girl! Sometimes I can't get that idea out of my head, and then I'm afraid that thinking about it so much, will *make* him appear." I swallowed hard.

Jesse leaned forward, reached across the counter and took both my hands in his. After a minute, he started talking. "Sara, I don't think old Rasputin is a daytime kind of guy. In your dream, he's always... *always*... tied up on a cot, right?" I nodded. "Ghosts or spirits, whatever, generally don't come with props like cots and such. There's not many places in this house where a ghost could actually fit an entire cot." I smirked a bit and he continued. "Sometimes, when something's really bugging me, I make a pact with myself to only think about it at a particular time of the day. Thinking about it at an alternate time is not allowed. I'll say to myself, 'no that issue will have to wait until eleven tomorrow morning for me to ponder it.' Maybe you could try something along that line? Have a designated Rasputin worrying time... in the morning or early afternoon... and try to train yourself not to think about him at any other time. You can always phone or text me if you need a distraction."

As I studied his face, his expressive eyebrows raised up slightly in a question. I realized he had calmed me, that his very presence calmed me.

"Okay, that's a good idea to try. And I feel much better just telling you about it too."

"I aim to please, ma'am," he drawled with a cowboy accent, and took a swig of beer. "You can unload on me any time… call me in the middle of the night if you need to."

We put the popcorn in the microwave and I asked if he remembered that *The Little Mermaid* was my favourite Disney movie.

"Of course… wouldn't forget something important like that." As I laughed, he added, "Brandon and Maggie own pretty much every Disney movie ever made, so if there's another one you'd like to see sometime, they probably have it."

We started with *The Little Mermaid,* and under duress, Jesse had to admit it was great. By the time Grandma and Grandpa returned home we were part-way through *Shrek.* They wandered into the TV room and shook their heads at our movie choice.

After inquiring if they'd won any prizes that night, Grandpa lamented, "Nope, your Grandmother was a sorry disappointment in that regard. I guess we go without lunch tomorrow."

After I explained the history of the joke to Jesse, Grandma added, "Well, your Grandfather came really close to having the lowest score, and then we at least could have come home with a roll of toilet paper."

We all laughed and then Grandma and Grandpa headed to bed. As they shuffled off, they informed us that a nice slow, steady rain had started.

Chapter Seventeen

few days after the movie night, Jesse asked about going to see Uncle Ray. "I went to Harrison Park in Owen Sound with Scott and the kids once, and I was wondering if we should go there. We can get a take-out lunch at the chip wagon, then sit on a bench at the river's edge and watch the swans and paddle boats, which might be less awkward than sitting in a restaurant."

"That's an amazing idea," I said.

"Okay, good. I'll talk to Scott and see what day would work best to go."

Two days later, the three of us were sitting in the sunshine on a park bench at river side, munching on fries and hot dogs. We watched a pair of swans swimming with a string of five baby swans between them, mother leading the way and father bringing up the rear.

"I wonder what a baby swan is called?" I said.

Ray was leaning forward, watching the birds intently, and quietly answered with, "Cygnet."

Jesse and I raised eyebrows at each other and then I asked, "Do the mother and father have special names?"

"Male is cob," Ray said. "Don't know term for the female."

"Well, why don't we find out," said Jesse. "Google will know." He did a search on his phone and determined that a female swan was known as a pen.

"Cob and pen," I said doubtfully. "I think I could have come up with better terms than that." But Ray repeated the word "pen" with interest and seemed to catalog the information.

After eating, we decided to follow a trail through the forest for about fifteen minutes and came out further down the river, near the park's mini-golf. Jesse asked if we should play a game, and after some thought, Uncle Ray agreed.

We got through the first eleven holes without incident. Both Jesse and Ray were beating me, of course. Ray still had not smiled, and talked very little, but he appeared well-focused and a bit more relaxed than usual.

But during hole twelve, Ray repeatedly and nervously glanced off to his right, then faced forward, gave his head a vigorous shake, and glanced to the right again. This behaviour continued through holes thirteen and fourteen. I was getting edgy, and exchanged several glances of a worrying nature with Jesse.

During the fifteenth hole I finally asked, "Uncle Ray, are you alright?"

Ray stood still, looking down at the ground, then gave a quick glance to the right and looked back down at the ground. In a very low voice, he asked, "Do you see children over there?"

Holding my breath and keeping my eyes on him, I said, "Uncle Ray, I do not see any children." He nodded slowly several times, still looking at the ground. "What are the children doing, Uncle Ray?"

"They have their hands out, like they're begging, but they say nothing."

I didn't know whether to query him or not, but decided to forge ahead. "So the medicine you're taking doesn't help? Does your doctor know you're still having these visions?" Somehow the term vision seemed better than hallucination, especially considering my own experience with my little ghost.

"The medication helps a bit. The visions aren't as bad. Usually it is just these children. I used to have more menacing visions."

Part of me didn't want to find out about the menacing visions, but I felt drawn to the information like a moth to a flame. I was also unsure whether to share my own "otherworldly" experiences with him. Would it be helpful to him somehow or just add to his burden?

After taking a deep breath, I said, "Uncle Ray, I sometimes see a little girl... sometimes in my dreams, but I've also seen her during the day a few times. She always just stands and looks at me and says my name. She seems very poor and very sad. Jesse and Beth think she's a ghost with unfinished business, and maybe needs me to help her in some way."

Uncle Ray slowly raised his head, turned towards me, and stared right into my eyes. I was startled. He had never looked me in the eyes before.

"I regularly see the same eight children," he said. "They're poorly dressed and look very sad. They reach out towards me like they want something."

It was surprising to hear Uncle Ray speak that much, and when he finished, our eyes stayed locked and we were both silent. Then he dropped the bomb.

"And sometimes the littlest girl says the name Sara."

My knees turned to jelly. Jesse tossed my putter to the ground and guided me to a nearby rock to sit down. Uncle Ray continued to watch me, and Jesse stood looking from me to Uncle Ray and back again.

"Are the children still here?" I finally managed.

Uncle Ray looked around. "No, they're gone."

"What does it mean?" I whispered, looking at Jesse.

"I don't know, but it's a connection." He paused and looked again at Uncle Ray and back to me. "Sara, I think you need to tell your uncle everything." I gave Jesse a long look, while Ray continued to study us both. "Come on,"

Jesse said, "there are picnic tables up front, let's go and sit down."

Jesse and I sat on one side of a table and Uncle Ray sat across from us. Hesitantly, I told him all about my nightmares and my little ghost. Uncle Ray listened intently, and to my surprise, he made frequent eye contact with myself and Jesse. After sharing everything except the "too many children" part, I stopped and looked at Jesse. He took my hand and nodded. "Your uncle deserves to hear everything." Running my finger along the indentations of "*Sandra loves Paul*" carved into the picnic table, I could feel them both watching me.

"Sara, what else?" Ray asked. It was probably the first time he had ever said my name or asked me a question.

Continuing to run my finger repeatedly over the carving, I took a big breath. "Uncle Ray, a long time ago, you got very upset at a big family gathering at the farm. You said stuff like 'too many children, too many mouths to feed.'" He didn't respond and I kept my eyes on the table "The thing is Uncle Ray... that Rasputin guy in my nightmare... he says that too."

Raising my gaze, we stared briefly into each others eyes. Then, still looking at me, he stood up slowly, shoved his hands into his jacket pockets, turned around, and took a few steps towards the fence surrounding the mini-golf. I was scared he might have some kind of break-down right then and there, but he stood quietly for a few minutes with his back to us, then sat back down at the table.

"I have seen your Rasputin," he said softly.

The two of us locked eyes. My heart and head were hammering, but I said nothing. Ray crossed his arms on top of the table and looked back and forth between Jesse and I.

Jesse was the first to speak. "This is incredible. It can't be a coincidence... it has to mean something. There has to be a reason for all of this." Then he explained that we had entered all the relevant information in a document and that he felt sure it was all related somehow. "It's like a bizarre puzzle that needs to be solved."

Ray nodded slowly. "Can you send me that document?"

"I'll do it tonight."

Later, when we returned to the group home, I walked with Uncle Ray up the steps to the porch then turned to face him. "Are you alright?" I asked.

At first it seemed that he wasn't going to answer. He took two steps towards the door, then turned half-way back around. With his eyes aimed at the floor he said softly, "I think you have given me hope, Sara." Then he turned, opened the door, and was gone.

That evening, I lay in bed awake for a long time with the events of the afternoon repeating in my mind. The part that actually bothered me the most was Uncle Ray saying I had given him hope. What if it was false hope? What if I let him down? And what if I followed his pathway? My brain was stuck in a useless rewind and repeat mode, and finally sitting up with a huff, I said out loud, "Maybe some fresh air would clear my mind. I'm not supposed to be thinking about all this in the middle of the night!"

After throwing off the covers, I hurried down the first

stairway and tugged open the door to the front balcony. A magnificent starry display greeted me, and stretching my arms up towards the heavens, I filled my lungs with the fresh night air. To the north, the big dipper dangled over the pond, and after a few minutes of scrutinizing, the little dipper also emerged. Turning around, I was surprised to find a full moon hanging high in the southwest. It looked gigantic, and the brilliant glow blocked the light from other stars in a wide area around it. It was spectacular.

Unlike many people, I had never been able to envision the features of a human face on the moon's surface, and assumed others just liked to perpetuate the myth about "the man in the moon." It really didn't need a face; it was stunning without one.

"Moon," I whispered, "my Uncle Ray said I gave him hope. But what if I can't help him... or even help myself? What if I let him down? It's so much responsibility to give someone hope." I sighed, scanned the sky, then looked back at the moon.

And suddenly, without any effort on my part, I saw a face in the moon. It was crystal clear... and it was smiling. The Man in the Moon was cheerily beaming down at me. Grinning back at him in delight, I said, "Hey, Moon, is that you being hopeful?" After breathing deeply a few times, and with my eyes still on the glowing sphere, I added, "Okay then, Moon, I'll be hopeful too... it's decided." Before long, my eyelids grew very heavy and I groggily shuffled my way back upstairs. It's possible I was asleep before my head touched the pillow.

Chapter Eighteen

*I*n the middle of July, Beth and her husband Cory came to the farm for the weekend. Saturday was cloudless and hot, and by one-thirty, other family members had started to congregate for some fun in the sun. Stacy, Scott, Maggie, and Brandan arrived, with Jesse's yellow Jeep right behind them. The kids disembarked dressed in bathing suits, and charged towards the water, dragging pool noodles and a large blow-up dragon, while life-guard Scott trailed behind with towels.

Stacy's parents arrived with a van full of family: her teenage brothers, and her sister with two pre-school boys in tow. Food was hauled to the kitchen, and coolers were lugged to the pond lawn. Grandma and Grandpa settled into their favourite chairs under the birch tree.

It was exciting to have Beth and Cory meet Jesse, and it turned out the four of us got along really well. We played a game which involved trying to throw frisbees into a two-level stand, and after much laughter and silliness, Beth and I beat the boys by an embarrassing (for them) margin.

Before long, a two-generation volleyball game broke out, with an older and younger generation cheering from the sidelines. After three rowdy games, we took our sweaty selves to the water, and of course, a diving/ jumping contest ensued at the diving board. This included the little kids (in life jackets), and involved significant quantities of shrieking and belly flops.

When things calmed down, Beth and I sprawled on beach towels on the grass, while Jesse and Cory each planted a lawn chair in the water directly in front of us. We chatted and sipped cold drinks. Since the swim area sloped into the pond, the guys' chairs eventually settled into the sand with a considerable backwards slant. It was too much to resist, and with some encouragement from their dad, Maggie and Brandon managed to sneak up from behind, tip the balance, and both guys flipped backwards into the water. Although their heads went under, they both demonstrated a burst of athletic skill and kept their beer above the water. The crowd howled and clapped, and the kids were rewarded with tosses into the pond by Jesse and Cory.

At four-thirty, Scott and Jesse headed down the road for evening milking, with Cory going along to assist. Beth and I helped clear up the afternoon's debris, and then went for a walk.

"So, Jesse seems really nice…" Beth said as we made our way to the barn.

It was a question without a question and I enthusiastically launched into a comprehensive account of Jesse that continued all the way back the lane. We stepped into the edge of the last field and realized there was a small flock of wild turkeys scratching about on the other side of the field. After noticing us, they started running towards the far bush, and Beth and I couldn't help but laugh.

"They look so ridiculous… like they're going to fall on their faces any second," Beth chuckled.

"They really do, and yet despite being the most awkward runners ever, they still choose to run rather than fly." The absurd creatures disappeared into the bush and we turned back towards the house.

"I'm so pleased for you, Sara," Beth said. "Jesse's pretty adorable, and you guys seem really good together. Cory and I are going camping up on the Bruce Peninsula the last weekend in July. You and Jesse should come with us."

"Oh, that would be so much fun, but I don't know, Beth. We've really only gone out on two actual dates. Mostly we just see each other here or at Stacy and Scott's place. We haven't even kissed yet. I think it would be weird to invite him to sleep in a tent with me."

Beth pondered this. "Okay, so what if I emailed you both about joining us and in the email, I'll just say that the girls will sleep in one tent and the guys in another... what do you think? Then you two don't have to angst over the whole tent thing and the idea comes from me, not you."

I thought it was a solid idea.

Back at the house, we helped get supper organized, and before too long the guys returned. A couple hours later, with dusk settling in, our overstuffed selves gathered around the campfire with beer, wine, and tea. Scott and the kids walked around the pond and lit the tiki lamps, and everyone admired the double display of flames—one set along the pond edge, with a second set of wavy reflections on the surface of the water.

Grandpa shuffled into the cabin and returned with several packages of sparklers, resulting in shrieks of excitement. Soon dancing kids wove light into the darkness. The teenage cousins suggested a sparkler race, and several of us rose to the challenge. This tradition involved running around the pond to see who could go the furthest before their sparkler expires. The three teenagers—plus Jesse and Beth—all circumnavigated the pond twice before their sparklers flickered out. The rest of us straggled behind.

By ten o'clock, the crowd dissipated, Grandma and Grandpa were escorted inside, and then Beth, Cory, Jesse, and I returned to the campfire. The frog orchestra was in full swing and the stars were so bright it seemed we could reach out and touch them. Before long, the guys started mumbling about hotdogs, so Jesse and I went to gather the necessary ingredients from the house. As we left the campfire, he took my hand, and in the middle of the lane he tugged me to a stop, turned to face me, and ran his hands up through my hair on each side of my face. The full moon gazed down at us over his shoulder and for a moment Jesse studied my face like he needed to memorize it. And then he kissed me.

Chapter Nineteen

The next morning, Beth and Cory headed back to the city. After lunch, I took myself out to the shade of the big birch and settled down to read more of Great Grandma Sadie's diaries.

London, England | 1914-1918

The Sunday after war was declared, Sadie and Walter went for a long walk in Kensington Park. They admired the gigantic Prince Albert Memorial, Queen Victoria's shrine to her beloved husband.

Sadie gazed at the seemingly endless carvings and statues that were part of the monument. "There is so much to look at... the details are astonishing."

Walter nodded absentmindedly, but then he turned her

around to face him and clasped both her hands in his.

"Sadie," he said and paused to search her face. "I'm very fond of you. I really enjoy spending time with you, and, well, I'm hoping you would agree to be 'my girl.'"

Sadie broke her gaze with him, stared briefly at the ground, then looked back up to his face. "Walter, you're a fine chap and I do enjoy your company, but I really don't want to get serious with anyone right now. I'm thinking of making some changes in my life and I'm not even sure I'll stay in England after the war."

He looked stricken. "What do you mean, not stay in England? That's ridiculous. Where would you go? And anyway, you can't go travelling off by yourself."

"I'm sorry, Walter, but I need to sort some things out for myself." Then she tried to change the subject, but Walter refused to engage in any more conversation, and he fumed the entire way home.

At the end of August, news reached London of the British retreat following the Battle of Mons, and in the second week of September, Walter signed up. When he shipped out, Sadie walked with him to the train station. He held her close in a tight hug, then pulled away and looked into her eyes.

"I love you, Sadie. Please wait for me. Maybe we can make plans to travel somewhere together."

"We can talk about it all when you come back, Walter. Now you be careful. Keep your head down and your helmet on. Write to me." She did not say she loved him. She waved until the train was out of sight, and four weeks later his first letter arrived.

Dearest Sadie,

I have come to understand that I am not a brave man. I am terrified here all the time. I'm terrified during every waking minute, and I'm even terrified in my dreams. Most of the time, I feel like my mind is not even connected to my body, like I'm sleepwalking or something. I do what I'm told, but I don't really understand what is happening. I live in wet ditches and bunkers. Young men, boys really, are dying all around me. Boys with parts missing from their bodies. Boys calling for their Mum and Dad. Boys sobbing in the night. And there are other boys dying in other ditches that I have helped to kill. War is madness, Sadie.

Sometimes I try to block out everything from my mind and just focus on you. I picture your beautiful smile and think about the good times we've had together. But I can't hold on to these thoughts for more than a couple minutes. I wish I had a picture of you. Lots of other blokes have pictures of their girls.

Please write and tell me what is happening in London. I will indicate below where to send a letter. I don't know how long it takes for the mail to get back and forth, but I will be hoping to hear from you soon.

Love Walter

When Sadie wrote back, she told him, "*Bravery doesn't mean not being scared, Walter. Bravery means you do what needs done, even though you are scared*." She sent him a photo of herself.

In Walter's second letter which arrived at the end of November, he wrote, "*I like your definition of bravery and if you're right, then I must be one of the bravest blokes in the world, because I'm always terrified.*"

Walter was killed the following March. Sadie knew he would be. He died in the Battle of Neuve Chapelle, along with thousands of other young British soldiers—boys she had gone to school with, boys she had cheered on at football games, boys who had a different idea of what war would be like.

On the night of May 31, 1915 Sadie was woken by Agnes shaking her. She had lit a candle.

"Sadie, I can hear a droning sound in the distance."

"An aeroplane?"

Agnes shook her head. "No, it doesn't sound like the aeroplanes we've heard before. And it's getting louder."

"We'd better wake up Mum and Father," Sadie said, and the girls snatched up their wraps and woke their parents. They went out to the street where neighbours were already scanning the sky. The droning sound became so loud that Sadie could feel the vibration.

Then, out of the darkness loomed a ghostly, floating monster. It was a Zeppelin. They knew Zeppelins had dropped bombs along the Norfolk coastline in January, and desperate fear surged through the family as they processed what they were seeing and the imminent danger.

"We have to go to the cellar!" Sadie screamed, but her father started marching down the street, shaking his fist towards the sky and yelling something she couldn't make out. Sadie looked at her mother who shook her head, indicating it was no use going after him.

Agnes seemed to be frozen in place, staring skyward in horror. As large as a warship, the Zeppelin hung in the sky above them. "Agnes, we have to go!" Sadie yelled, grabbing her sister and dragging her inside and down the cellar stairs, where the three of them clung to each other.

The droning eventually grew somewhat dimmer and seemed to move south. "Probably heading towards the docks," their mother, Hattie, whispered.

The first explosion suddenly ripped through the night and the house rattled but remained intact. For the next four hours the three women huddled in the cellar, trembling and listening.

By daylight the skies were silent, and the three women crept back upstairs and peered out the windows towards the street where a few people were already gathered. Without saying a word to each other, Sadie and Agnes drifted outside and started asking people if they had seen their father. By late morning they found him unharmed, asleep on a park bench a few blocks away.

After they returned home, Agnes reported to the family, "People are saying that large crowds went to see the damage in the bombed areas of the city. But apparently some of those mobs deteriorated into anti-German rioting. There was looting of shops and businesses with German-sounding names. A chap told me his friend had seen a sign posted on one shop that read 'WE ARE RUSSIANS.' I guess their Russian name might look German, and they were trying to save their business."

Several people were killed on that first night of bombing, and after that night, Zeppelins became a regular terror in the skies of London. Over the next many months, Sadie and her family spent several nights in the basement of their house. Sometimes the girls' father went down with them, sometimes he stayed upstairs, and sometimes he went out to the streets, but regardless, he always "preached" throughout each bombing. His rants did not involve words of comfort or inspiration, but actually escalated feelings of helplessness and terror in others.

"Behold, the day of the LORD cometh, cruel both with wrath and fierce anger, to lay the land desolate: and he shall destroy the sinners thereof out of it!"

In July, Sadie's father lost his job at the docks due to his obsession with the Bible and his escalating instability. An old friend who had worked with him for many years came to see Sadie's mother.

"I am sorry to say that your husband is unreliable, unproductive, and at times quite dangerous at work," he explained. "Some of us have been trying to cover for him for a while, but I'm actually surprised he wasn't given the boot earlier. How are you and the girls managing with him? Has he ever seen a doctor?"

After the man left, Sadie and Agnes pleaded with their mother to speak to a doctor, but she just shook her head and walked from the room.

The Battle of the Somme began in July 1916 and went on for many months. The British and French slowly gained ground on the Germans, but the cost was horribly high. On the first day alone, almost twenty thousand British soldiers were killed. In the following months, Sadie described the casualty numbers in her diary as "*staggering, inconceivable, impossible to comprehend*"—and the war ground on.

In 1917, a new hell rained down on London as the Zeppelin bombing was replaced by aeroplane bombing. To add to the terror, Sadie's father grew more violent at home, attacking Hattie on several occasions, leaving her bruised and bleeding. Then one evening, he attacked Agnes, and it took both Hattie and Sadie to pull him off. The following day Hattie convinced a doctor to came to the house, and the girls' father was diagnosed with Religious Mania. The next day, a paddy wagon pulled up in front of the house, and three constables took him away in handcuffs.

"I curse you all to eternal damnation," he raved. "You will all go to Hell and be punished for time without end!" It took all three men to wrestle him into the vehicle.

Sadie's father was committed to the Stone Sanatorium at the north end of the city, and for a while, Sadie's mother went to see him once a week. A few times, Sadie and

Agnes asked to join her, but their mother forbid it. Three months later, the doctors told Hattie that her visits made her husband more violent, and it would be better if she stayed away. Hattie seemed relieved.

On Wednesday, June 13, 1917 just before noon, Sadie felt the whole factory shudder; she immediately locked eyes with Maisy across the room. The machines ground to a halt as everyone stopped working. Sadie silently mouthed, "What?" to her friend, who mouthed back, "Bombs!" and she raised her hands high and brought them down sharply.

For the first time, London was being bombed in the daylight. Maisy darted over, grabbed Sadie's hand, and they ran to the stairway which was quickly packed with workers. Some people yelled, "Get to the basement!" while others screamed, "No, go to the street!"

While Maisy and Sadie struggled to get to the main floor, the building shook two more times, resulting in screams from the panicked crowd. Sadie yelled to Maisy, "I'd rather take my chances outside than be crushed by three floors of the factory!"

When the two friends finally reached the main level, they followed a few others who were climbing out through a window, rather than wait behind the mob pushing towards the door. Outside, Sadie and Maisy shoved through the crowd, trying desperately to find Emma. It was a surreal, daytime nightmare, with the skies seemingly filled with dozens of airplanes. Even Sadie could hear the high-pitched scream of the bombs and feel the shudder of each explosion from the far side of the city. The landscape shook, and terror clawed at the air around them. Heavy smoke rose over the East End like a gigantic evil apparition. When the bombing finally stopped, Sadie and Maisy started to shakily walk home, as there was no point trying to get a tram. An hour later, they caught sight of Emma further up the street, and ran to catch up. The three of them collapsed into each others' arms, crying with relief.

Over the next couple of days, it was reported that 162 people died in that raid, with hundreds more injured; and to the horror of the populace, Upper North Street Primary School in the East End had been hit. A bomb fell through the girls' class on the third level, continued to fall through the boys' class on the middle floor, and then finally exploding in the infant class on the ground level. Eighteen children died, most between the ages of 4 and 6 years, and dozens more were seriously injured.

The following Saturday, Sadie and Agnes went to the East End to attend the funeral procession for fifteen of those children. Fifteen horse-drawn coaches, completely enveloped in flowers, passed by the solemn crowd on the sidewalks, en route to the East London Cemetery and a mass grave. Sadie cried through the entire procession, cried all the way home on the tram, and cried for an hour afterwards in her room. Walter's words from his letter written almost three years earlier, repeated over and over in her head, "War is madness."

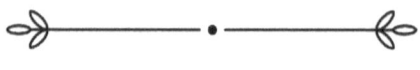

In February of 1918, with a small feeling of optimism, Sadie recorded in her diary, "*Women over thirty have been given the right to vote. It appears that war has done more to move forward women's rights than all the speeches, fire bombs, hunger strikes and marches put together.*"

From the beginning of the war, women had "*taken up the mantle*"—working as police, railway guards, bus and tram conductors, firefighters, and bank clerks. They operated heavy machinery and worked in dangerous munitions factories, and it was finally decreed that they were also capable of making an informed choice in an election. Well, at least the women over 30.

The war ground on, but by the summer of 1918, the English populace were slowly becoming aware of a new terror: the Spanish Flu. In early September, there were reports at the boot factory that three people from the second floor had died from the flu. Then a few days later, Sadie arrived home very distraught.

"A man on our floor," she whispered, "yesterday he seemed perfectly fine when he arrived in the morning, but by lunch time he had turned all purple and was sent home. We found out he died before supper last night!" Sadie felt more exhausted than terrified, numbed by the previous four years of war.

Hattie hugged both girls tight to her and in a choking voice asked, "How can we bear more? How can we endure more suffering and death?"

But endure it they did. As the death rate soared, Sadie convinced her mother and sister to follow the lead of some others and wear bandages over their noses and mouths, especially at the factories or in crowds.

By November a new word was being used in the newspapers: pandemic.

Chapter Twenty

Rural Ontario | 2005

On a Wednesday morning near the end of July, I was outside searching for Grandpa with a goal of corralling him towards the computer screen. The three of us skyped with Mom and Dad in London at least once a week, and Mom had texted earlier to alert me of an eleven o'clock Skype call. Grandpa was at the workbench in the shed with some unidentifiable item in the vice grips.

Twenty minutes later, both grandparents were sitting in front of my laptop while I stood behind them. Mom and Dad appeared on the screen, with Mom laughing at something, and shaking her head so that her brown bob swayed back and forth.

"What's so funny, Mom?"

She quipped a line I'd heard more than once before. "Oh, you know your father... he's so full of shit that his eyes are brown."

Dad then appeared on screen with a devilish grin on his face, and leaned in so his mop of curly dark hair clung to the side of Mom's head. Since moving to London in January he had grown a salt and pepper beard plus a moustache, and I still wasn't quite sure these additions suited him. Mom reached for her glasses and settled them on her face. She owned several different pairs, and that day had chosen the vibrant blue frames, which popped the navy blue of her eyes.

Grandpa spoke first with his standard query. "Well, what's happening on your side of the pond?"

We did the usual catching up of events in both locations. Mom and Dad were happy about the upcoming camping trip with Beth and Cory, and were also very pleased that I had applied to local school boards. They were intrigued about Great Grandma Sadie's diaries and I gave them a brief overview, including that Sadie had pretty much lost her hearing, obviously from the noise in the factory, although it didn't seem that either she or her doctor had made that connection.

"I'm definitely interested in reading those diaries sometime," Mom said. "Hey, I went to a very interesting restaurant the other day. It's a perfectly charming little inn and a friend and I had lunch outside on a little terrace set amongst some ancient apple trees. It was just lovely, but what was most interesting is that apparently the inn has a resident ghost. Our waitress told us it's a little girl, claimed she has seen her four or five times, and that some overnight guests had seen her as well. Apparently, the little girl doesn't really do anything, just looks sad and then disappears."

Mom was aware of my little-girl dreams, but was unaware I'd seen her in the daytime as well. Apparently, she had not noticed the similarity between the ghost she described and my dream girl, and I didn't point it out to her.

"Hmm, sounds interesting," I said, then changed the topic. "Well, it's a smoking hot day here, and Jesse and I are going to the beach this afternoon."

"Ah, good for you," Dad said. "We're both looking forward to meeting Jesse… if you haven't abandoned him to a sad and lonely, non-Sara existence by the time we return,"

"I'll try to keep him around for a while longer, Dad."

Jesse and I planned to stay at the beach until evening. The second-cut of hay had been completed the previous day, so farming life was briefly less hectic (until harvest time for the wheat, about three weeks later). By one o'clock, it was scorching hot. I was wearing my black bikini with a purple and mauve cover-up. I had somewhat successfully French braided my hair into one heavy plait, and was in the farmhouse entranceway slathering myself with sunscreen. Jesse drove in and I gathered up my bag and sunhat, slipped on my purple flip flops, and called goodbye to Grandma.

When we arrived at Sauble Beach, we left our gear in the Jeep and went for a walk. Once on the sand, I kicked off my flip-flops and delightfully dug in my toes. But after a couple steps, as the bottom of my feet started to sear, I realized my mistake, and with much yelping, charged ahead to the cool relief of the water.

Laughing, Jesse caught up. "Rookie move," he said and removed his shoes while standing on the wet sand. He took my hand and we strolled along, watching a parasailor while the waves rhythmically washed over our feet.

"I didn't dare tell Maggie and Brandon we were coming to the beach," he said.

"Oh, good thinking," I laughed, but we agreed to have a beach day with the kids another time.

"So we skyped with Mom and Dad this morning," I said, "and Mom told us an interesting ghost story." Then I related the details she had shared.

"That sounds a lot like the little girl you see, doesn't it?" Jesse said.

"Yeah, it seems spooky little girl ghosts are really prevalent these days."

We were back near the car and retrieved our towels, my bag, the little cooler Jesse had brought, and then took ownership of a chunk of beach. After spreading out our towels, and stripping down to bathing suits, we ran towards the water. Jesse dove in immediately, and when he surfaced, started vigorously splashing me, which quickly aborted my usual slow-entry style. With a shriek of protest, I dove. We swam, splashed, laughed, bantered, and finally headed back to our towels. When Jesse was lying peacefully on his back with closed eyes, hands behind his head, skin warm and dry, I wrung out my braid over his bare belly. He roared in shock. I outran him for about three paces, before he picked me up, headed towards the water, and dumped me in. Back at the towels again, he watched me carefully as I innocently wrung out my hair over the sand and then laid down on my towel.

My bag was propped under my head so I could view the waves and beach action. A nearby young mom gave some snacks to her kids, and immediately a half dozen seagulls magically appeared overhead. They swooped and hovered, rarely moving their wings, their undersides astoundingly white against the sapphire sky. Within minutes the children started tossing bits of bread into the air, and with limited disputes and impeccable timing, the gulls swooped down to catch each tidbit. After the last toss, the family packed up and trooped towards the parking lot. A couple of the gulls shot me dubious, sideways looks, decided I was foodless, and winged out over the lake into the endless blue.

Late in the afternoon, we returned most of our stuff to the car and walked to the beachside patio. Jess ordered a beer and I decided on a piña colada. As we sipped our drinks, he looked out across the water, and a little frowny, squinty bit developed around his eyebrows while his lips rolled inward.

"Is something wrong?" I asked.

"No, no, I'm just thinking about that little girl ghost your Mom told you about. Did she say anything about what she looked like, or whether she spoke?"

"Nope, I told you everything Mom said about her. Why?"

"Well…" he took a sip of beer, set the bottle down slowly, and gave it a little twirl back and forth. "I'm just kind of wondering if it could be the same little girl that you and your Uncle see."

Setting my glass on he table, I stared at him. "What do you mean? How could that be?"

"I don't know," he said. "It's just kind of nagging at me. Could you ask your Mom to find out more information? What she looks like and whether she says anything?"

"If I tell her the reason she'll think I'm really going crazy."

"Well, give it some thought. It just seems like a very weird coincidence to me. But anyway, let's get some menus and order dinner."

Later that evening, I phoned Beth and told her about my great day with Jesse, about Mom's ghost story, and about Jesse's thoughts on the ghost story, as well as my own reservations.

"Sara, Jesse is right! You have to find out more about that little ghost at the inn. The universe has handed you a piece to the puzzle. There must be a million restaurants in London and there's a reason Mom went to that particular one, and that reason is the ghost. And I doubt that every waitress talks to their customers about the ghost, but Mom got the waitress who did. It's a connection Sara, an energy reaching out to you. This could be the first step in solving everything."

My thoughts were scrambled and I didn't respond.

"Sara?"

"Okay, okay, I'll email Mom right now and let you know what she says."

Once the email was complete, I went to bed. It was the middle of the night in London, so Mom wouldn't answer until at least tomorrow. After about an hour of tossing around in the bed, I finally threw off the cover and sat up with a huff of exasperation.

And there she was, standing in front of the west window. Immediately, I froze and just looked into her eyes. The term "depths of despair" crept into my mind.

Swallowing hard, I said in a shaky voice, "I want to help you. I'll try my best, but can you tell me what I should do?"

Of course she could not. All she could do was repeat my name three times and break my heart with her overwhelming sadness. Then she faded away and left me watching as the high branches of the maple tree reached northward with the wind.

Three days later, I sat nervously in front of my laptop at Grandpa's desk. Still slightly in shock that Mom had arranged an actual Skype call with the waitress from the inn, I had recruited Jesse as backup, and he sat right beside me. He had previously peppered me with questions about every detail of the little ghost's appearance, and had a pen in his hand and a list sitting on the desk.

Right on time, Mom's face appeared on the screen. She introduced us to Molly the waitress, who was a middle-aged, plump woman with a very pale and very expressive face showing an abundance of laugh lines. She was wearing a bibbed white apron and an old-fashioned maid's cap over her hair, with brown curls peeking from under the edges. I thanked her for staying late after her shift.

She laughed excitedly. "I'm just as pleased as punch to talk about our wee girl with you, dearie. What would you like to know?"

Before long, we learned that the little ghost at the inn had been hanging around for decades. Molly said the child appeared to be 3 or 4 years old, and her clothes indicated poverty. Jesse checked off these matching points on our list.

"So what does she actually wear, Molly?" I asked.

"The poor mite is in bare feet with a dress that looks a couple sizes too big for her and is quite dirty," Three more check marks. "Her hair is long and unkempt... just scraggly all around, kind of dirty blonde, I would say."

Check and check. Jesse pointed with the pencil to "rip in dress?"

"Molly, what colour is her dress, and did you notice any rips in it?"

"I think her dress is just a dirty brown… with a bit of faded gingham pattern to it. And yes, there's a rip in the dress," Molly continued, "right in the front, a pretty big rip with a chunk of fabric missing. You can see a different layer of fabric underneath."

Suddenly I felt like I was drowning, and I grabbed hold of Jesse's knee as if it were a life preserver. He covered my hand with his own and gave it a squeeze. The last point on our list was "Does she speak?" I could feel my mouth trying to form the words but no sound came out. Jesse knew I was struggling, so he filled in by telling Molly what a great memory for detail she had, and how much we appreciated her help. Finally, he told her we had one more important question.

Taking a big breath, I asked, "Molly, does the little girl speak?"

"Well, yes, she does. I was getting to that, but it seems so weird. She's only ever said one word." Molly paused, chewed at her lower lip a bit and glanced at my Mom.

We waited until I could stand it no longer. "She says Sara, doesn't she, Molly?" I blurted out. "The only thing she says is my name."

Molly looked straight at me and her eyebrows lifted up close to her curls. "Yes, sweetheart, that is what she says. Over and over, so sadly it seems her wee heart has broken right apart."

My vision suddenly went black and it felt like I was

falling… hurtling down a dark, bottomless tunnel. Then I felt the warmth of Jesse's arms circle around me, and distantly heard my mother calling my name. Gradually, the room and the screen came back into focus. I felt shaky and cold, and rested my forehead on the desktop, while Jesse rubbed my back.

"Sara, are you alright?" my mother asked… once, twice, maybe more.

Finally, I sat up and nodded, then explained about the room going black, and the falling sensation. Jesse still had one arm around me and looked at me with concern.

"But Sara, sweetheart," Molly asked, "How did you know what our little ghost says?"

"It's one of my recurring dreams. She just stands there looking sad and forlorn and repeats my name." I didn't say the little girl also came to me during waking hours.

"How close was Molly's description to your dream girl?" Mom asked.

Jesse held up the list for them to see that every point had been checked off.

"It's the exact same child," I whispered.

Chapter Twenty-One

On Monday, November 11, 1918, Sadie wrote in large letters on the top of her diary page, *PEACE AT LAST.* There had been rumours and false announcements in some papers over the previous few days, but at last the Prime Minister had officially announced at eleven in the morning that the Armistice Agreement was signed and *"the war to end all wars"* was over.

Immediately after the announcement, people swarmed out of shops, homes, and factories and took to the streets. Sadie, Maisy, and Emma hugged and cheered amidst the crowd in front of the boot factory. Church bells near and far rang out the joyous news.

"Let's go to Trafalgar Square!" shouted Maisy.

"Yes, let's do it!" Emma agreed.

But Sadie was horrified. "No, we need to get away from the crowds, not mingle with new and bigger crowds. Think of the risk. It's not worth it. We can go to my place and celebrate together there."

"Oh Sadie, don't be such a wet blanket! This is huge. I'd always regret not going down… and so will you."

Despite Sadie's continued objections, her two friends headed off downtown without her. During her tram ride back home, Sadie was amazed that hundreds of flags of all sizes were already hanging from windows and balconies along her route. Children ran through the animated crowds, blowing bugles and waving hand banners. Once home, Sadie sat on the front porch with her sister and mother and watched the people out on their street.

The next morning, Sadie arrived at the tram stop early to buy a newspaper, and she studied photos of Trafalgar Square and Piccadilly Circus from the previous day. Multitudes of people had covered every inch of Trafalgar Square, with men waving flags and hats while standing on the backs of the bronze lions. The photos showed buses and trams stranded like beached whales, unable to move amongst the sea of people, with soldiers clinging to the sides and perched on the tops of the marooned vehicles.

Soon Maisy and Emma rushed up to Sadie, babbling with excitement to tell her all about the celebration. Sadie was glad to see her friends, but felt more disheartened than excited. The paper said that 124,000 young British men would never return from the war. England was full of wives and children who would never see their husbands and fathers again, and countless young women would never marry and have children because their generation of men had been practically annihilated. The lives of the wounded would never be the same as before the war— both the physically wounded, and the poor souls who suffered from "shell shock" and who seemed to live in a state of perpetual terror. But Sadie tried to hide her own uncertainties as her friends and the general populace were in high spirits. Even the Flatau brothers who owned the boot factory decided not to dock people's pay for leaving their stations the previous day.

At five-thirty the next morning, Sadie and Agnes were getting ready for work when Agnes heard frantic pounding on the front door. They both rushed down the stairs. Upon opening the door, they were shocked to see Emma gasping for breath with tears streaming down her face. Sadie moved forward to hug her and guide her inside, but Emma stepped back, waved her away, and between ragged breaths gasped, "No, don't come near me!" Then she collapsed on the floor of the porch still waving at them to stay away. Sadie wrung her hands ,waiting for the blow of this latest disaster—the news she was already guessing—hoping against hope she was wrong.

"It's Maisy," Emma gasped. "She died from the flu

about two hours ago. Her brother phoned." Emma dissolved into ragged tears.

Sadie's family did not have a phone, so Emma had ran the ten blocks to Sadie's house through the dark cold morning. Sadie clutched Agnes and they sank to the floor. But Agnes soon darted off and returned carrying blankets, wrapping one around Sadie and tossing another to the shivering Emma.

"I can't," she started to say, but Agnes quickly interrupted.

"You can take it with you, Emma. You're freezing." By then, Hattie was up and made tea, and Agnes used a piece of kindling to push a cup towards Emma.

After a couple of sips, Emma whispered, "We should have listened to you, Sadie… we never should have gone. And when we got there, Maisy insisted we take the bandages off our faces, saying we looked ridiculous, and that almost no one else was wearing them. I took mine off too, Sadie," and she started sobbing anew.

"Emma," whispered Sadie, "you know sometimes members of one family die and others in the same household live. Don't give up hope."

Emma nodded vacantly. "I should go." She rose unsteadily, tightened the blanket around herself, and locked onto Sadie's eyes.

"If you don't come to the factory tomorrow, I'll come to your house after work to check on you," said Sadie, and when her mother started to protest, she added, "I'll knock on the door and then stand at the bottom of the outside steps just to see you how you're doing."

Emma nodded and gave Sadie a last, long look before turning away.

In the end, the Spanish flu killed twice as many British people as the war. Many children were kept home from school for months. Buses and trams were sprayed with disinfectant twice a day. Unbelievably, the pandemic swept around the entire globe, and in some countries, handshaking and spitting were outlawed.

But Emma survived, as did Sadie, her sister, and her mother. Emma was dangerously ill for four days, and every evening after work, Sadie knocked on the door of her friend's house and walked back down the outside steps before the door opened and Emma's mother passed on her report. On the fifth day, when Sadie got to the bottom of the steps and turned around, Emma herself stood in the doorway, grinning weakly.

By the spring of 1919, the pandemic in Britain had dwindled to a few scattered cases. For those who were left, life went on. In April, Sadie proudly received her first union card, a small pink folder proclaiming her as a Woman Member of the London Metropolitan Branch of the National Union of Boot and Shoe Operatives. The government enforced minimum hourly wages, which were not the same for men and women, but were still an improvement in the earnings of women.

In June, a pilot successfully flew from Newfoundland

to Ireland and the papers predicted transatlantic passenger flights in the near future. Sadie however, thought this was preposterous.

"How could an aeroplane company make money flying a couple people across the Atlantic? It's not possible."

That summer, Sadie and Emma, along with Agnes and her friend, Jane, started to once again frequent the Electric Cinema which was under new ownership and had been renamed The Imperial.

It showed three different double bills a week, requiring weekly decisions about which show to attend. Sadie in particular loved the theatre, as she did not feel disadvantaged by her deafness, although she greatly missed the musical score. On Sunday afternoons, the young women often put together a picnic and went to Kensington Park or the London Zoo. The girls sometimes persuaded Sadie to bring along her copy of *My Man Jeeves* by P. G. Wodehouse, as her straight-faced readings and amusing accents generally reduced them to gales of laughter. But despite the rhythm of normal life returning, Sadie felt unsettled.

"*I so miss Maisy's relentless 'joie de vivre', her impetuous charging at life, and her infectious laughter,*" she wrote in her diary. "*And I constantly feel jittery and on-edge, almost like I'm waiting for another bomb to fall, waiting to hear more bad news, waiting for some further catastrophe to occur. At night in bed I lie awake for hours, feeling tense and twitchy. I just don't know how to calm myself.*"

Chapter Twenty-Two

Rural Ontario | 2005

It was the last Saturday in July. Beth and Cory had arrived at the farm the previous evening and by nine thirty in the morning, the three of us were headed north on the County Line.

We popped into Stacy and Scott's place to pick up Jesse, who added another tent, cooler, and duffle bag to the pile of gear in the hatch of the car. It was a clear, hot summer morning, and we were pumped.

After twenty minutes, we were at the base of the peninsula that divided Georgian Bay from the main part of Lake Huron. Initially, cedar and pine forest crowded the road on both sides, then the landscape opened up to scatterings of small farms valiantly holding back the bush. Some of the farmsteads appeared shabby and exhausted, overwhelmed by the poor soil, harsh winters, and the never-ending rocks that grew like bad weeds on the land.

By late morning, we arrived at our campsite in Cyprus Lake Park, about fifteen minutes below the tip of the peninsula. When we climbed out of the car, a trio of hyperactive chipmunks were engaged in a wild chase game all over the area.

"Looks like this site is already taken," Scott said, and we all laughed.

An hour later, the tents were up, we were dressed in bathing suits and t-shirts, and the guys had shouldered day packs containing lunch, sunscreen, and towels. We cut across the campground, walked along the near edge of a small lake, clattered across a bridge, and headed out on the trail to Georgian Bay.

"Just smell that cedar," Beth remarked and we all inhaled deeply of the spicy, rich fragrance.

After thirty minutes, we emerged from the forest onto bare rock, and the four of us stood like conquerors on high cliffs overlooking the edge of the bay.

"Wow, this is outstanding!" exclaimed Jesse. "Look how the water near the shore is so pale, but then it drops in depth and changes to a completely different colour."

"So many blues," I added. "Pale turquoise, vibrant cobalt, and then at the horizon it meets up with the sapphire sky. Amazing."

To our right and left stood magnificent, sculpted, overhanging cliffs. The whole panorama was breathtaking.

"Look at how far those cliffs are cut in," said Beth.

"Do you think the one we're standing on is like that too?" We all looked at each other and slowly moved backwards a few steps.

"So I looked it up," Jesse said. "The bottom of the cliffs are soft limestone and have been carved for centuries by wave action. I think the harder capped tops are dolomite." Jesse was a bit of a researcher and liked to share.

We scrambled along the rocks until we found ourselves looking down at the famous Grotto, which is a large cavern, partially under water.

"So we need to go down," Beth declared. I looked at her skeptically, but she continued. "We can either climb down the cliff wall, or the shorter way is actually down this tunnel." She walked over to a hole in the rock surface. We all peeked into a narrow vertical tunnel, which basically went straight down through the rock and opened to the cavern below.

"I'd just like everyone to know I'm not a fan of either of these options," I stated, but they all pointedly ignored me.

"Well, the tunnel's a lot shorter and is so narrow that you couldn't really fall far," said Jesse. "The cliff looks riskier to me... how far do you think that is?"

"The cliff wall? Maybe around twelve metres," said Cory. "I vote for the tunnel too."

Jesse went first, leaving his pack topside, and I followed. It was nerve racking at first, but within a couple minutes, I came to terms with the dark tight space, and shimmied my way down. Jesse gave me a high five when I emerged, grinning.

We all sat on the rock edge, and hung our legs into the water. There was a collective gasp, and Cory said, "This is barely above freezing!"

"Yeah, the water is much warmer on the Lake Huron side of the peninsula," Beth said. We all gave her piercing looks, and she defended herself saying, "But this side is prettier!"

Eventually, with yelps and shrieks, we all made it into the water… briefly. Afterwards, we clambered up the cliff wall, which looked considerably less scary from the bottom than it had from the top. Further along the trail, we found a private spot to have lunch.

Pointing at the square-ish chunks of grey rock tumbled over the shoreline, I said, "They look like the building blocks of a giant toddler."

After lunch, we returned to the trail and traipsed across Boulder Beach, a cove completely filled with round rocks. An hour later, satisfied with our day, we retraced our steps back to the campground.

When we reached the campsite, it was almost six o'clock, and we soon were enjoying some cold beer and the chilli I had made the previous night.

As we finished up, Jesse said, "Too bad we can't see the sunset over the water from this side of the peninsula."

"Nope, we can't," Beth agreed. "But you can see it from the other side, and the peninsula isn't very wide up here. Pebble Beach is just a little further north on the west side. It has a great sunset view."

"Oh, okay," Jesse said. "So should we go over there? Sara loves a sunset over the water."

"Oh, yes, great idea," I agreed.

But surprisingly, Beth shook her head. "Well, I'm actually pretty beat and quite comfortable here. Why don't you two just take the car and go on over?" She then gave Cory a little elbow jab, and after a slight pause, he stood up and fished the keys out of his pack.

"Yeah, you guys should go. We'll stay here and start a fire." He tossed the keys to Jesse, who headed toward the car. I rolled my eyes and shook my head slightly at Beth, who grinned and gave me two thumbs up.

As the name would imply, Pebble Beach was pebbly. Grabbing an old blanket from the car, we crunched our way towards a huge weathered log, bleached the colour of eggshells. We sat on the blanket and gazed over the water, which was absolutely calm and flat. I couldn't believe no one else was there.

Heavy gold clouds weighed down the western sky, and the sun quickly disappeared behind them. A few minutes later, it dropped below the clouds and a scarlet strip stretched along the horizon, while a perfect mirror image floated on the water below.

The bright strip vanished, and the clouds broke up and drifted away in puffs of gold and coral. A water-colour canvas was left behind, with pastel shades melding in the sky and rippling over the water. I soaked it all in, but eventually felt Jesse watching me. He was turned my way, with arms crossed and head cocked, seemingly deep in thought. When I met his eyes, he smiled and pulled me close.

When we arrived back at the campsite, there was a fire going, hotdog fixings organized, and an open bottle of red wine. Cory poured wine into four plastic glasses, which we raised up high while Beth said, "Here's to making memories."

As we tapped the glasses together, I weirdly got a catch in my throat and felt my eyes filling up. I took a shaky big breath, and silently scolded myself for being such a sap.

We settled around the campfire and started telling stories about previous camping trips—good and bad. Around midnight we all crawled into our respective tents and I fell asleep, still smiling.

Suddenly, I gasped and sat straight up in the pitch black, feeling completely disoriented and breathing heavily. "Where is she? Where is she?!" I swivelled my head and groped around. "Where's the little girl?"

"Sara, what's going on?" It was my sister's voice coming out of the blackness.

"The little girl," I gasped, "Where is she? What's happened to her?"

"You were dreaming, Sara." My sister's warm hand rubbed my back. Then she turned on a flashlight and the walls of the tent emerged, with our duffle bags piled in one corner and the netted doorway at the end. Turning to my sister, I reached for her hand, and took in a ragged breath.

"You're shaking," she said. "I didn't think the little girl dream was this upsetting for you. Aren't the other two the bad ones? Are you okay?"

"It was different. She was different." And I took a ragged breath. "Her voice wasn't that mournful monotone like always before. She was more agitated, urgent, desperate. And her face was contorted, afraid. It was the face of terror, Beth. What am I going to do? This has to stop!"

Beth continued rubbing my back and holding my hand. Finally, she said softly, "Sara, I really think the little girl is stuck in some kind of limbo, between this life and the afterlife, and she comes to you because she somehow needs your help."

"But what does she want me to do?!" I wailed. "I don't know how to help her or to help myself!"

"Well, I've been thinking about this," Beth spoke slowly and carefully, as if afraid of saying the wrong thing, "and I really think the key to all of this is in London. You need to go to London, Sara, and to the Three Sister's Inn. There is some kind of connection, a missing clue, over there.

"I can't go to London. How could I possibly know what to do there?"

Beth squeezed my hand and continued, "I've already checked my work schedule and I could go with you in September if you wanted me to. There just has to be a way to make sense of all this. Maybe the Three Sister's Inn holds the answer to the puzzle."

The idea of going to England was overwhelming to me. "I don't know," I whispered.

"That's okay," she said. "You can think about it for awhile, maybe everything will become clearer somehow." She squeezed my hand and then reached to open the back flap of the tent. "You know, it's just after five and I can't imagine either one of us going back to sleep. Why don't we take the flashlights, walk out to the shore, and watch the sunrise?"

Still breathing hard, I turned to stare at her and said nothing. She sensed my negative vibes and responded as if I had spoken. "No, really, we should. The sunrise will be amazing and it will clear your head."

"*Might* be amazing," I finally said, and after a pause. "You're really serious, aren't you?"

"Come-on, come-on, come-on," she said in sing-song—a respectable imitation of my favourite childhood persuasive chant.

Sighing, I gave in. "Okay. Let's do it." After rummaging in the bottom of our sleeping bags for clothes, we bumbled our way through the campground and started gingerly up the trail, shining our flashlights ahead. Except for the birds, we were the only foolhardy souls up at that time of day. After forty minutes, we emerged from the forest into faint light and stood on the cliffs perched over the bay. We reached for each other's hand, gingerly walked closer to the edge, and sat down cross-legged. Subtle light leaked from the far horizon where water met sky.

After a few minutes, mauve clouds heralded the coming sun which then peeked up over the horizon in a blaze of orange. It continued its orange ascent and momentarily balanced on the water's far edge with a widening streak of orange rippling across the bay towards us. We watched in silence as the fiery ball rose higher and slipped behind a mauve mountain range of clouds, with sundogs of light streaking heavenwards from the mountain tops. A moment later, the sun peeked through a rip in a cloud, tore it further apart, and indigo patches floated carelessly away. The colours in the water and sky quickly faded until it seemed they were never there at all. Two seagulls swooped through the new light.

"Amazing," I whispered.

"Really amazing," Beth whispered back, as if we were in church or something. And maybe it actually was God's church, maybe God never intended churches to be built of stone and wood. Then Beth added, "I told you so."

At seven-thirty, we headed back down the trail, and just as we entered the forest, Beth's cell phone rang. It was Cory, and Beth explained that we would be back in about half an hour. When we arrived at our camp, the boys had pancakes and sausages ready, with maple syrup plus tea and coffee. Best breakfast ever. We told them about walking through the dark forest and tried to describe the sunrise. They appeared suitably impressed.

But after a few minutes Cory asked, "So did you guys plan this? Did you set an alarm or something?"

"Well, no," Beth said, while I tried to give her a meaningful look, which she meaningfully ignored. "Sara actually had a bad dream and we both woke up."

"Oh, Sara, I'm sorry," Jesse said, and put his hand on my shoulder. "Which one was it?"

So with Beth's encouragement, I reluctantly described the dream and the escalation of its overall tone. Jesse and Cory asked a couple of questions and then there was silence.

Jesse was frowning a bit, and had his lips clamped together. It was his pondering face so I knew something was coming. "Sara, I think you need to go to London," he said.

Beth practically yelped. "That's what I said! I even offered to go with her!"

"Really?" Jesse said. "That would be fabulous!" And they all looked at me.

Looking at the ground, I slowly shook my head. "But I don't have a clue what I would do, where I would go, who I would talk to?"

They continued badgering me until finally I agreed to think about it, just to have some peace. But a pretty convincing voice in my head kept saying, "No, no, no."

Chapter Twenty-Three

The following day was Monday. Beth and Cory left for the city and there was nothing urgent for me to do, so I settled myself on the pond lawn with the next instalment of Great Grandma Sadie's diaries. The sun was valiantly trying to maintain supremacy of the sky, but appeared to be loosing the battle, as sinister clouds slowly advanced from the west. A crow flew above me and squawked out a harsh, gritty alarm, but if he was forewarning a storm, I thought he was a bit premature.

It was Sadie's second to last diary. The war had been over for fourteen months and Great Grandma had plans.

London | 1920

In late January, Sadie announced her intentions of emigrating to Canada. Her mother and sister were heartbroken and tried to dissuade her, but Sadie was adamant.

"There are too many dreadful memories in England. I need to clear my head of the war, the flu, the death. London is the largest and most prosperous city in the world, and I know in my heart it's only a matter of time before England will be in the midst of another war. I want a fresh clean start, and Canada is a long way from European powers. I'm sorry, but this is something I have to do."

"How can you think of such a thing?" wailed her mother. "Have you forgotten the Titanic? It's not safe. You're being irrational, Sadie."

"Mum, ocean travel has become much safer *because* of the Titanic tragedy."

"There will still be icebergs out there somewhere. And Sadie girl, you're deaf!" her Mother tried a different tact. "How can you possibly travel all by yourself?" But Hattie knew in her heart this was a weak argument. Sadie was a very competent and mature young woman, and by lip-reading she could keep up with a group conversation.

Sadie declined responding to her mother's last point. "I'm going, Mum, but not for several months. In order to save more money before leaving, I'll book a passage for the end of the summer."

Sadie purchased passage from Liverpool to Montreal on the R.M.S. Pretorian of the Canadian Pacific Ocean

Services, leaving Liverpool on the 31st of August and arriving in Montreal on September 5th. As the time drew nearer, the days sped up. Summer was quickly upon them and Sadie started doing her 'lasts'…. the last time she would go to the zoo with her sister, the last time she went to the cinema with Emma, the last time she strolled around Trafalgar Square, the last time she fed the swans on the Thames river.

On Monday, August 30th, Sadie, her sister, and her mother all took the train to Liverpool where they stayed at an inn overnight. The next morning, they rose at four, and arrived at the dock at five. After hugs and tears, Sadie walked up the gangplank and away from her old life forever.

On the Pretorian, Sadie hauled her belongings down two flights of stairs, found her cabin, and introduced herself to Mrs. Belwood, a lively older woman who was her roommate.

"My Henry, bless his gruff old soul, he was taken by the flu in '18. Last summer, I went and visited my son and his family in Toronto, and they've persuaded me to go and live with them. So here I am, off on a big adventure… at the ripe old age of 60!" And she laughed heartily at herself.

Sadie immediately liked the woman, but unfortunately Mrs. Bellwood suffered from sea sickness during the first couple of days. It didn't help that their small, windowless room was below water level. Sadie had no such problems, and spent most of her time walking the decks, breathing in the fresh ocean air, and studying the wide array of travellers on the ship. At regular intervals, she went downstairs to check on Mrs. Bellwood, hauling her bucket down the hall to rinse, and fetching her fresh water. On the third day, she helped Mrs. B up the stairs to the fresh air, and she started to gradually improve.

Sadie felt guilty about leaving her mother and sister, but hoped she could convince Agnes and maybe even her mother to emigrate to Canada over the next couple of years. She tried not to think of her father, but it was difficult to keep his image out of her mind.

About two weeks before she had left London, Sadie went to the sanatorium to say goodbye to her father, knowing she would never see him again. Sadie's mother told her not to go—even tried to forbid it—but Sadie was adamant. From the outside, the San appeared well-kept with lovely large lawns, although they were suspiciously unoccupied. But as soon as Sadie stepped inside the building, all loveliness disintegrated. An overpowering smell—which seemed to be a combination of human feces and disinfectant—greeted her at the door. A nurse at the front desk seemed surprised when Sadie said she was there to see her father, but she provided directions to find him and Sadie set off down the hall with trepidation pounding in her chest. She passed by several large rooms, all of which were crowded with poor, senseless souls, sitting unseeingly in chairs or shuffling about mindlessly. One older woman was cuddling a doll. Some of the inmates were muttering to themselves, or yelling out, and occasionally she caught the note of a high pitched scream.

Eventually, Sadie found the correct room. It had three rows of five beds, with most beds unoccupied, and there was Sadie's father in the middle row, lying on his back, confined with a straight jacket, and tied to the bed with a strap around his waist. He was half sitting up and straining at the stays, swaying from side to side as he shouted and raved. His hair and beard were long and matted, and his eyes were crazed, unfocused. The stench was overpowering and Sadie kept her handkerchief over her nose as she tried to decipher her father's rants.

"What have you done?" he shouted, without seeing her. Spittle drooled down into his filthy beard. "Your sister's blood is crying to me from the ground! Now you are cursed, cursed, cursed FOREVER!"

Sadie tried to interrupt his raving, to catch his attention. She yelled out "Father! It's me Father... it's your daughter, Sadie!" But he showed no recognition of her, and Sadie sobbed out loud, whispered goodbye, then turned and fled.

Chapter Twenty-Four

Rural Ontario | 2005

*M*y breathing had stopped. With eyes wide, I stared, unblinking at the diary page, then heard an anguished, strangled, animal sound, and realized it was coming from me.

Rasputin! Rasputin was my great, great grandfather! I knew it was him, it was an exact description, but how? How was it possible? HOW WAS IT POSSIBLE to have nightmares about a man I never knew existed?

A loud crash of thunder right over my head made me jump and the diary tumbled to the grass. I stared down at it blankly but couldn't get my brain into gear. The crow screamed another warning, and there was a splitting display of sheet lightning on the northern horizon.

Shuddering, I slowly reached down for the diary, put it under my shirt for protection from any raindrops, and stood up. Feeling unbalanced, I turned and headed slowly towards the house. Raving Rasputin was my great, great grandfather! What could it mean?

As I went through the door, Grandma called out from the backroom, "We're having some tea, bring a cup if you'd like some."

"Thanks, but I'm going upstairs to read a bit more," I managed to say, hoping they couldn't hear the panic in my voice.

"Well, if the storm gets too bad, come on back down."

After a shaky walk through the kitchen, I lowered myself onto the bottom step of the staircase for a few minutes. My mind was in chaos, but eventually I climbed the stairs in slow motion, walked down the hall like a zombie, and plodded up the second set of steps.

The rain had started in earnest by then. Feeling as though I might shatter like crystal with any sudden movement, I carefully laid back on my bed and watched as large drops of rain exploded on the sky-light above. The drumming of the rain matched the pounding in my head and the question that repeated itself like a circular sound bite: *What does it mean? What does it mean? What does it mean?* I dozed off.

Forty-five minutes later, I woke up. It was still raining and my mind was still on Great Grandfather Rasputin. But now I knew one answer to the question.

It meant Beth and I were going to London.

Chapter Twenty-Five

*F*lights to London were booked for the second week of September. Beth could only take a week off work, but Mom persuaded me to stay longer and join her on a two-week road trip into northern England, with brief excursions into Wales and Scotland. Thinking about the entire expedition gave me heart palpitations, so I concentrated very hard on not thinking about it at all.

That first week in August was heavy with humidity, and even the ever-exuberant birds and cicadas seemed dulled by the oppressive heat. Grandma had cabin fever from spending several days inside the air-conditioned house, so to distract her, I invited Jesse for dinner.

Grandma perked up and made tea biscuits for strawberry shortcake, emphatically stating, "Any strawberry dessert made with angel food cake or pound cake is NOT strawberry shortcake."

I had always loved grandma's strawberry shortcake, so was quick to agree (while savouring a mouthful of warm biscuit and melted butter).

"Also," she added, as she reached into the fridge for her chilled bowl and beaters, "none of that disgusting stuff that comes out of a spray can. It has to be homemade biscuits, strawberries, vanilla ice cream, and proper whipped cream."

Nodding enthusiastically with my mouth full of a second biscuit, I rummaged in a drawer for the engine end of the beaters. The steak was already marinating, and as Grandma revved up the beaters, I started preparing vegetables. Jess would barbecue the vegetables and steak—nothing like inviting a guy to dinner so he can cook it! Grandpa made a special trip to town for a bottle of red wine and was so pleased with himself, I couldn't tell him that neither of us liked red wine.

At the beginning of dinner, we caught up on the current state of farming—we needed rain; the second cut of hay was sparse; Scott would be bringing two more calves down the next morning. Then Jesse asked Grandma and Grandpa how long they had lived on the farm.

Grandpa responded with, "Got a calculator?" and we all laughed. "Well now, we came here in '47, so I guess that would make it fifty-eight years." Jesse marvelled at the time span, while I marvelled at Grandpa's math skills.

"So did you move here right after you got married?" Jesse asked.

"No," he said, looking at Grandma, "We were married almost five years before we moved here, right Red?"

Grandma smiled and her green eyes sparkled at his use of the old nickname, "We got married the last day of '42 and moved here in March of '47, so four and a bit years."

"I have two questions," said Jesse. "First of all," and he looked at Grandpa, "did you just call your wife Red? Secondly, you got married on New Year's Eve?"

Grandma sniffed. "Well, we were supposed to get married on the second last day of the year, but somebody was twenty-four hours late for his wedding."

"What?!" Jess blurted out and looked at Grandpa.

"I had some 'splainin' to do," quipped Grandpa, which apparently was a frequent phrase on the old *I Love Lucy* show.

So Grandma and Grandpa launched into a favourite family story: their wedding. They were married in 1942, about half-way through the Second World War. Grandpa had enlisted immediately after his eighteenth birthday, so had been in the air-force for almost two years by then, was trained as a flying instructor, and stationed in Gander, Newfoundland. Grandma lived with her two older sisters in Toronto at the time, and worked in a munitions factory. The wedding was to take place on December 30th, at the beginning of Grandpa's two week leave. He had a long ferry trip, however, and then a very long train trip to reach his bride, and the weather was uncooperative. A huge snow storm in the eastern provinces delayed the trains for hours and hours.

"I was to meet him at the train station and then we would go directly to city hall," Grandma said. "Just my two sisters and my cousin George would be there. Anyway, I got to Union Station and there was no one to answer questions, but the arriving trains were hours late, so I figured it must be a snow storm. After waiting for several hours, I finally went home again."

"You didn't call her on your cell phone to let her know?" exclaimed Jesse, and we all laughed.

"So," Grandma continued, "we ended up getting married the next day, when the groom finally arrived on the scene, and that was New Year's Eve."

"And people have always provided a bang-up anniversary party ever since!" Grandpa added with a grin.

"Not long after we were married, he got stationed in Saskatchewan, and we lived in a little house close to the base. That was the winter there were three or four plane crashes, killing the student and instructor. It was very scary." She shook her head slowly.

Grandpa added, "Yep, the wings folded right up over the damn cockpit, trapping the instructor and the student inside. They had no chance of ejecting with a parachute before the plane crashed."

"That's horrible," I said and everyone nodded solemnly.

"It was pretty bad," Grandpa continued, "and it took a while to figure out the problem. Finally, they determined that the glue used in the wing structure could not tolerate the extreme Saskatchewan winter temperatures and it just gave way."

"Wow," Jesse said. "Incredible."

"Well, that was a long time ago now," Grandma said, and started piling up our empty plates.

"So were you stationed in Canada for the whole war?" Jesse asked.

"Pretty much," said Grandpa. "Close to the end of the war, myself and most of the flight instructors were sent to England…mainly because there were so few men left to teach to fly. But the war ended shortly thereafter, and I never was sent to battle. Say Red," and he looked at Grandma, "Remember S.W.A.K.?" Grandma repeated the letters a couple times and looked at him blankly. "Oh, come on," he teased, with twinkling eyes, "I can't believe you don't remember."

Grandma shook her head. I knew from experience that Grandpa would not give it up, so I decided to write down the letters for her… S.W.A.K. She took one look and said, "Oh, of course… Sealed With A Kiss," and shook her head at Grandpa again. "We always put that at the end of our letters to each other."

As I smiled at them both. A sudden choke in my throat welled up, and I quickly started clearing the table. Jesse helped build the strawberry shortcakes, which to Grandma's delight, Jesse loved. Partway through dessert, Grandpa back-tracked to Jesse's other question, and explained that Grandma's red hair had earned her the nickname Red when she was young.

"That's a great nickname." Jesse said, then looked at

me and raised his eyebrows, "So Ginger, can you make biscuits like Red here?"

We all laughed and I assured him I could not. We then played three games of euchre, with Grandma and Grandpa winning two out of three, fair and square.

I was eager to tell Jesse about the little girl dream from the previous night, so after dinner, we went for a walk. "It was so weird, because in the dream, I took a picture of her. She was standing in a room with flowered wallpaper."

"Like a picture with a camera?"

"Well, with my cell phone, actually."

"Huh, interesting. Maybe your mind is trying really hard to remember the details of her. Was the wallpaper like in your room, with the little blue flowers?"

"No, the wallpaper in the dream had big pink and mauve flowers... a bit gaudy. Google informed me this morning that they were probably zinnias... not sure if I've ever seen zinnias in real life."

"Well, you've never read the Bible either, but that doesn't prevent you dreaming about it."

"Right. But the part that really bugs me is that I can't remember what she said. It's like viewing a film clip with the sound off. In my mind her lips are moving, but I don't know what she's saying. Maybe she said something really important."

Jesse took my hand and gave it a squeeze. "Or maybe, you want more information so badly that you conjured up this dream, but there is nothing else to learn right now.

Perhaps your dream didn't actually have any sound. The information you need will come to you... somehow. But maybe you need to clear your head of it all for awhile."

We turned back towards the house and saw that dark rain clouds had congregated in the western sky, compressing the light into a narrow band of orange along the horizon, while completely blocking out the sun above. But as we watched, the sun sank into that open strip, and by some trick of light refraction, suddenly presented as two fiery orange suns stacked one on top of the other. It was a surreal and somehow unsettling image that only lasted for a moment. Then the two blazing balls merged into one, and dropped below the horizon.

The rest of August scooted by in a blur. Early in the month, I went to Markham with Jesse for the weekend and met his two brothers and his dad. On the same weekend, my dad returned from England to do holiday coverage at the optometrist office, so I stayed with him for a week and stocked the fridge and freezer, as he was always a bit helpless and hopeless without my mom around. That Friday, Beth and Cory took me back up to the farm, and the four of us went to a great beach dance in Port Elgin. Jesse rated it as "outstanding."

Twice in August, Jesse and I hauled the canoe down to the river and went fishing, and the second time we actually caught some brown trout. We also took Maggie and

Brandon for a beach day late in the month, and had a blast. Wave jumping, sand castles, mini-golf, and ice cream— what's not to like?

At the farms, the grain was harvested from the wheat fields, leaving huge round bales of golden straw scattered throughout the fields—sentinels keeping watch over the land. Eventually they were hauled off and stored in one of the barns, or tightly covered by a wrapping machine and lined up outside into long, white, rounded rows, like tunnels to nowhere.

I had not picked up Sadie's diaries since reading her description of my great, great grandfather, and was apprehensive about learning any more inexplicable connections to the present day.

But Jesse encouraged me to keep going. "It's only a week until you leave for London," he said. "You need to finish the diaries. There might be more clues to help in your quest."

He was right, so one drizzly day in late August I picked up the last diary. "Okay then," I said to myself. "Let's do this." And I settled into the porch with a cup of tea.

Chapter Twenty-Six

Ocean Voyage between England and Canada | 1920

Often during her walking tours of the deck, Sadie's thoughts returned to her family, especially to her father. She didn't want the last image of him to be at the sanatorium, and wished she hadn't gone. Having cried all the way home, she was met at the door by her mother and sister. While describing her visit, tears rolled silently down her sister's face, and her mother's lips set into a grim line. Eventually, her mother had made them all tea and the two girls started asking questions about their father.

"Why did you decide to marry him, Mum?" Agnes asked. "What attracted you to him?"

"Well, it will seem strange now, but part of my

attraction was because he was a church-going, God-fearing man who did not touch the drink."

The two sisters looked at each other and shook their heads sadly.

"And back then, he was a hard worker with a good job at the docks," Hattie added. "Your father refused to have any of his family at our wedding ceremony, saying they were evil and drank too much. I couldn't even convince him to invite his mother, although eventually I insisted we visit her occasionally. We never saw anyone else from his family. He had two brothers and a sister that I never even met."

"I never knew that, Mum," Sadie said. "But was he a nice person when you were first married?"

"Well, I think he was, actually. But when you girls were tots he started to go a bit off kilter, and then over the years he became more and more difficult.

"So Mum," Agnes pushed, "most families have several children. We always wondered about there being only the two of us."

Hattie sighed. "Well, that was your father's decision. He told me from the beginning that we would only have two children. He said he would not give life to children he could not take care of properly. He was adamant, so we took all the precautions we knew of to prevent a third pregnancy."

The girls were surprised by this information. "Why do you think he was so adamant about it?" Sadie asked.

Then Hattie told the girls what she knew about their

father's early life. "His family was dirt poor, even poorer than my family, and we barely managed. Your father's father worked at the docks, but he was a drinker and his pay often didn't make it home. Then, when Isaac was about 4, his father was killed at work. He was missing for a week before his body was found floating in the harbour. It was assumed that in his usual drunken state, he had fallen between the dock and a supply ship without anyone noticing."

"Oh, how awful," whispered Agnes.

"So your grandmother was left with six or seven small children and no income. She took in laundry to make a bit of money, but often there was no food for those children."

Sadie interrupted her mother's story. "Is that why Father would sometimes rant about, 'too many children, too many mouths to feed?' It never made any sense because there was just Agnes and I."

Hattie agreed that her husband had probably been referring to his birth family. "I imagine his mother could have often lamented in that way. I saw the children once in a while, especially in the fall, over at the spinsters' orchard."

The girls queried this and Hattie explained. "On the other side of High Road, when we were children, there was an apple orchard owned by an elderly gentleman and his three spinster daughters. They all lived in a large house on the edge of the orchard. You know where the Orchard Pub is on High Road?" The girls nodded. "Well, that used to be the family home. Anyway, after the old man died, the sisters allowed neighbourhood children to gather fallen apples in their orchard, and we all used to do so in the autumn. Actually, your father and his little sister were gathering apples there the day the little girl disappeared."

Sadie and Agnes looked at their mother with renewed interest. "What do you mean, disappeared?"

"Well, when your father was 5 or 6, he and his younger sister went to the orchard, but somehow he lost track of the little girl and eventually arrived home alone. Many people searched for the child, but she was never found." Hattie concluded with, "Your father, of course, kept this all to himself, but one time his mother told me about it."

Sadie asked, "So if Father was 5, how old would the sister have been when she disappeared?"

"Oh, I expect she was 3 or 4," her mom answered. "She was probably stolen away or killed under a carriage, I suppose."

Rural Ontario | 2005

Looking up from my reading, I studied the swaying willows. From behind the barn, the swooping sounds of "killdeer, killdeer, killdeer," floated as the bird emphatically repeated his own name. This new information in Sadie's diary did not alarm me. It was almost like I expected it. Of course Uncle Ray's troubles with "too many children" had a connection to our family's past. Of course the little girl who visited me held a role in my ancestral history. Of course.

Chapter Twenty-Seven

It was the beginning of September and I hadn't had a nightmare or a ghost sighting for almost a month. Jesse and Beth thought my ancestors were not bothering me because they knew of my upcoming London trip—that I had listened and was going to do something to help them. What that something would be was still a mystery to me.

Beth however, seemed confident. "A course of action will become clearer when we're in London," she stated with apparent conviction. I emphatically hoped she was right.

Jesse was about to start his last year at York University and would commute from his father's house in Markham. I had two interviews set up with the Grey County Board of

Education during the following week, both being maternity leaves that started late in the fall. The previous week I had attended two interviews in the city, but did not get either position.

"It's all part of a master plan," Jesse assured me. "It's not your destiny to live in the city."

Having finished reading all of Great Grandma Sadie's diaries, I had learned about her arrival in Montreal and the shock when she realized that virtually everyone spoke French. However, she still somehow managed to get a job at a boot factory, probably taking her little hammer and the shoe anvil to the factory to demonstrate her skills. I smiled to myself while reading the story Grandma had already related to me—that Great Grandma was unable to explain she could operate the "modern" machine under wraps in a corner of the factory.

After a while, Sadie met William, a young American man who was living and working in Montreal. A few months later Sadie became pregnant, but she wrote, *"William did the right thing by me."*

They were immediately married, moved into a tiny apartment, and seemed quite happy. But unbelievably, tragedy struck, and William never got to see their child. On his way to work one day, he was jostled by the crowd on the street, fell in front of an electric streetcar, and died instantly. I cried while reading Sadie's words of anguish and despair. She was eight months pregnant and completely alone. With no one else to turn to, Sadie ended up contacting Mrs. Bellwood, her cabin mate from the Pretorian, who convinced her son to let Sadie live with them until the baby was born. Alone, and with a broken heart, Sadie boarded a train to Toronto.

A few weeks later, Sadie lay in a Toronto hospital bed with her newborn child: Grandpa. Somehow, she got the idea that because she was deaf and had no husband, the nurses were going to take the child away from her. In response, she got herself dressed, picked up her son, and walked right out of that hospital. Thinking that the hospital staff might track her down if she went back to Mrs. Bellwood's family, she managed to find a boarding house. Sadie worked in the boarding house, and eventually the owner helped her find a job up north in Pyrite.

"Do you know the town of Pyrite?" I asked Grandpa.

"Oh sure, it's about an hour's drive east of here, near the Beaver Valley ski area. Named after a fair-sized 'gold rush' in the mid 1850s, but the glitter turned out to be "fool's gold" —or pyrite."

The Pyrite boarding house that Sadie lived and worked in was mostly rented to loggers. She worked long hours, often while carrying baby Grandpa in a sling. Around that time, a letter from her sister Agnes indicated their father had died in December 1923, from Religious Mania.

Eventually, one of the loggers, became interested in Sadie. Great Grandma wrote, "*Cecil said we should get married. He's a gruff man who speaks little and smiles less, but he says he's going to buy a farm, which would be a good place for little Eugene to grow up. I have a baby and I'm deaf, this might be my only chance.*"

In April of 1924, Great Grandma married Cecil and

they moved to a farm near Eastdale. Her diary entries became sparse, but she wrote that she fed and hand milked cows, cleaned out stalls, cared for chickens and gathered eggs—a young woman who had grown up in the "modern" city of London! She planted a huge garden and with instructions from her new neighbours, canned large quantities of fruits and vegetables. Soon after giving birth to a second son, Sadie wrote in her diary for the last time. "*I'm so afraid Cecil will find my diaries and burn them. I have to stop writing, and find a place to hide them all.*"

Incredible. What a life Great Grandma Sadie had lived, and the diaries only reported thirteen years of it! After that, she gave birth to two more children, moved several times, lived through the Great Depression in rural Ontario, and mourned the loss of her second son who never returned from Flanders Field in the Second World War. GG must have been made of pretty tough stuff. Eventually she had eighteen grandchildren and lived to know four great-grandchildren, including me. I was 3 when she died. It would have been wonderful to have known her, and to have learned more about her remarkable life.

It would have been wonderful too, if I had inherited some of her courage, tenacity, and strength. She went through so much in her life. Surely I could make this trip to London and successfully unravel the family mystery that quite literally haunted me.

"Great Grandma," I whispered, "I'll try my best. If my resolve becomes shaky, I'll think of you. Your bravery and resilience will bolster me."

Chapter Twenty-Eight

T he Saturday before I left for London, Jesse and I sat in the porch with all of Great Grandma Sadie's diaries on the table in front of us. He had brought printed copies of my family tree, and also of "Mystery Matters" as he called the document where we recorded any details that might be related to the little ghost or to my great great grandfather.

"I want to make sure we're not missing anything," Jesse said, as he laid out the family tree. His lips rolled inward and his eyebrows wrinkled in thought. "So, let's start with Great Great Grandfather Rasputin... the diaries never did give you his actual name, right?"

Shaking my head, I said, "No, Sadie only referred to him as Father. Too bad she hadn't included a family tree ."

"Clearly she wasn't thinking about future generations. Anyway, now that we know this man was your great great grandfather, it seems a little disrespectful to call him Raving Rasputin... so let's call him Triple G." I laughed and he continued. "Triple G was diagnosed with 'Religious Mania' and became completely dysfunctional, according to Sadie's accounts. Triple G's other daughter, Agnes," and he circled her name, "your great great aunt, did the 'out the window and around the house' routine while calling the name Sara. Then, there's her son, Tom," he circled that name then paused and further wrinkled his brow.

"Who was Grandpa's cousin," I prompted.

"Right, right," he nodded. "It seems that Tom was tormented by some kind of hallucination or contact from the beyond... which caused him to hurl himself in front of a speeding train. Your Uncle Ray (circled) definitely sees visions, including the same little girl you see. He also has seen Triple G, aka, Raving Rasputin."

Jesse then circled my name, scanned over the family tree, and with elevated eyebrows, looked at me.

"Yes, I see it," I said slowly. "There has been one individual from each generation since Great Great Grandfather, all the way down to me, who had something squirrelly going on."

He nodded. "Let's rephrase that, shall we? It appears that a couple of ancestors have been attempting to make contact with their descendants... seemingly a descendent from each generation."

We stared into each other's eyes, and then looked back at the family tree.

"This is not a coincidence," Jesse said. "This is a pattern."

I really hoped the pattern did not end up being schizophrenia, but I didn't express that concern out loud. Then Jesse wanted to read about the little girl who went missing, so I found the page in diary number six and handed it to him. He skimmed down and started to read out loud about the children going to the apple orchard on the day of the little girl's disappearance.

Suddenly he snapped his fingers. "That's it! Look here," he pointed. "It says the orchard was owned by an elderly man and his three spinster daughters. Sara, what's the name of the inn with the ghost?"

"It's the Three Sister's Inn." As the dots connected, I said it again slowly. "The Three Sister's Inn… the three spinster sisters!"

"Right," he said. "That's it. Something was nagging at me. That's it!"

"There might be something else," I said, and he looked at me earnestly. "The day Mom first had lunch at the Three Sister's Inn, they ate on the outside terrace, and I'm not sure, but I think she said there was an old apple tree on the grounds."

"That would be amazing," Jesse said.

We decided to call Mom right then and there to confirm. She answered immediately and since I rarely made an actual phone call, her immediate response was, "Sara, are you alright?"

"Yes, yes, I'm fine, Mom, but Jesse and I were talking about the Three Sisters' Inn. Did you tell me there were old apple trees there?"

"Oh yes, there were definitely a couple old apple trees around the terrace area of the inn. They were in full blossom that first day I was there… beautiful. But why do you want to know such a thing?"

Bingo. Thanking her, I promised a full explanation when I got there. After hanging up the call, Jesse gave me a high-five. "Outstanding work, Sherlock!"

Laughing, I said, "Maybe I'm Watson and you're Sherlock. You figured out the three sisters thing."

That evening, Jesse took me to Port Elgin for dinner and a sunset viewing. After eating, we walked along the edge of the limitless lake, and the sky did not disappoint. As the sun sank lower, streaks of fuchsia cut through a mauve sky. In short order, the bright globe plunged into the watery horizon, leaving behind tight layers of scarlet, fuchsia, and violet, stacked like flamboyant pancakes high into the sky, with undulating reflections mirrored in the water below.

Mesmerized by the magnificent display, I complained about not bringing my camera.

"You did," Jess said.

"Right! Am always forgetting I can take pictures on my phone."

After snapping several photos, a young couple came along and asked me to take a picture of them on their phone, and reciprocated by doing the same for us. As they wandered off, Jesse put both arms around me from behind, rested his chin on the top of my head, and together we gazed at the lake and sky. By then the colours had merged and softened, until the whole cloudless panorama was a gentle mauve that seemed to go on forever. That sunset felt like a promise somehow and I leaned into Jesse and pulled his arms tighter around me.

As we drove back to the farm, I pulled out my cell phone and began looking at the many, many photos of the sunset. The photo of the two of us was great, and I showed it to Jesse when we were at a stop sign.

"Yeah, that's good," he said. "Can you send it to me?"

"Definitely, if I just knew how."

Laughing, he said, "I'll teach you when we get back to the farm. And you'd better send me lots of pictures while you're in London."

Still scrolling through the photos, I suddenly clamped my hand on Jesse's upper arm and whispered, "Pull over."

He glanced at me in alarm, turned onto a gravel side road, and stopped the Jeep. As I handed him the phone, he looked down at the screen and his mouth dropped open. Then he turned his head slowly towards me and we locked eyes. Directly before all the sunset pictures on my phone, there was a picture of a ragged little girl, standing in front of a wallpapered background of large pink and mauve flowers.

In silence, we stared at each other while my heart hammered in my ears. He reached over and rubbed one hand on the back of my neck, then looked at the phone again. "Does she look the same as when you've seen her or dreamt about her?"

I nodded numbly.

Jesse squeezed my shoulder, still looking at the picture. "This is mind-boggling, unbelievable... and yet, here it is... this photo on your phone. Should I send it to my phone and print off the picture? Should you take a printout with you to London?"

Taking a big breath, I nodded and said, "But Jesse, let's keep this to ourselves, okay? Let's not share it with others right now. This is way up there on the weird scale and there's been some pretty freaking weird stuff already."

"Yep, I agree with you there," he said, and we heard a beep as the picture reached his phone.

Chapter Twenty-Nine

The day before our flight to London, my little ghost made a reappearance. I had just come down the attic stairs and was rounding the corner to walk to the second stairway, and there she was, standing in the hall in front of me, staring at me in profound silence. I crouched down to her level, and spoke to her softly. "I'm going to London tomorrow and really hope that's what you want from me. Can you tell me what to do there?"

She seemed to hold my gaze thoughtfully, and appeared to actually ponder the question. I tried to contain my excitement at the prospect of real information, while being careful to maintain my expression. Finally, she opened her mouth to speak. "Sara, Sara, Sara," she whispered, as if it were a secret—as if it were a message—and then she disappeared and I was alone.

That night, the coffin nightmare returned and woke me in the usual panic. While stretching out my stiff limbs and trying to clear my mind, I heard the little ghost girl say my name two times. While trying to regulate my breathing, I looked around the room and listened, but could not hear or see the child. Still trying to get my bearings, I swung my legs over the edge of the bed, stood up unsteadily, and walked slowly towards the west window.

A half-moon floated in the sky, while dark clouds rushed past it, heading north. Then my gaze was drawn to the lawn below, and there she was. The tiny girl had her neck bent backwards and was looking straight up at me. The bright moonlight made her as white as—well—as white as a ghost, and her tattered dress and tangled hair were swept to the north by the wind.

We stared at each other for maybe two minutes before her lips moved as she spoke my name…just once. Immediately, she seemed to disappear right into the ground as if a cavity had opened up below her. I stared transfixed at the empty spot, until eventually, my gaze shifted back to the sky where endless, inky black clouds still soared past the moon.

"Can you help me, Moon?" I whispered, "Will you be there with me in London?" Moon offered no solace, but backlit the old maple on the lawn as it swayed to the north, stretching towards something that was just out of reach.

The next morning, I woke up very early, abandoned all efforts to go back to sleep, and decided to go outside and witness the sunrise. After quickly dressing in jeans and a sweatshirt, I made my way downstairs in the soft darkness, then added a jacket from the front closet and pulled on my hiking boots.

The eastern sky was seeping light as I made my way to the west side of the pond, then turned to gaze over the water, towards the treed horizon. To my disappointment, the sky seemed almost devoid of colour, it just slowly grew paler and paler. The air was chilly and damp, my boots were soaked through from the dewy grass, and overall the sunrise seemed a bit of a bust. But then I started paying attention to the rest of the world around me. A constant hum of cicadas emanated from the surrounding fields, while a congregation of birds chattered and flitted about in excited anticipation. A dog barked in the distance, and a rooster from the farm on the hill repeatedly announced the coming of the sun, as if it were an urgent message.

Suddenly, I noticed with a bit of a jolt, that a drama was unfolding on the surface of the pond in front of me. A heavy mist rose from the shallow end of the water, then drifted past me northward to the opposite end of the pond. Astoundingly, the mist rose and moved like a procession of ghostly people trudging silently towards the far side, then disappearing over the edge. There were even a few child-size figures interspersed amongst the larger forms. It was a mesmerizing migration, constantly rising anew from the shallow water. Beyond the line of plodding apparitions, the eastern horizon grew brighter and brighter, until the dazzling edge of the sun emerged. Incredibly, this seemed to signal the masses, who suddenly changed direction, quickened their pace, and headed towards the sun.

Crowds of figures converged in the middle of the pond, then turned abruptly and streamed directly towards the light, apparently lured by the intense brilliance of the rising sun. Entranced, I watched the figures completely vanish, seemingly absorbed by the radiant light.

I felt dazed. Was this event some kind of spiritual rite of passage? An eerie, transitional ritual from the beyond? Was I somehow guided to witness this event, and if so, why? What did it all mean? What was I to learn? Or was the whole thing a figment of my imagination? Had my lack of sleep and anxiety about the trip caused me to transform common morning fog into ghostly apparitions?

Throughout the rest of the morning, I felt unsettled and twitchy, but I finished my packing and double checked my lists. The London flight was late evening, and Jesse planned to be at the farm just after lunch so he could drive me to the airport. By noon, I was hyper and fidgety, with both my head and stomach swirling in anxiety. I tried to imagine what would happen in England, and whether or not the trip would improve my situation or make things worse. What if the nightmares became more frequent or severe? What if I started seeing Rasputin in the daytime? What if I stirred up some completely new horror?

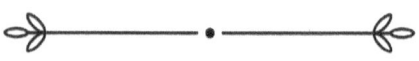

Jesse arrived right on time. My grandparents received hugs all around, then we packed my bags into "Little Miss" and headed her back to Toronto. We had arranged to meet Beth and Cory for supper at The Keg restaurant near the airport. As we waited for our food, Jesse and Beth talked excitedly about the last few "clues" that had been revealed in the final diary, and Jesse showed her the updated "Mystery Matters," as well as the family tree. They agreed that we first needed to determine where Great Great Grandfather had lived in London. They both looked at me, so I nodded and said, "Right," with more confidence than I actually felt.

After dinner, the guys drove us to the airport. I hugged Jesse hard, and then he put his hands on both sides of my face and gave me a long look. "You got this," he said.

Shortly afterwards, the two of us were soaring away from Ontario and towards England. Beth wanted to read the last two diaries, so I fished them out of my backpack, and also retrieved the envelope that held the little ghost girl's picture.

"Beth," I said, "I have something to show you." I paused.

"Okay," she said, a little warily it seemed.

"You know there's been some freaky things going on in the last few months." I took a big breath. "But I'll warn you, this might just be the freakiest."

"Okay," she repeated, definitely wary by that time.

"Three or four weeks ago, the little girl came to me in a dream. But it was different than usual because in the dream, I took a picture of her with my phone, while she stood in front of wallpaper that had big mauve and pink flowers. Jesse thought it was my mind trying to remember every detail of her. Then last week, when Jesse took me to the beach, the sunset was so stunning, I took a bunch of pictures on my phone."

My sister was studying me carefully, and was possibly holding her breath.

"On the way home from the beach, I was looking at the photos… and right before the sunset ones, there was a picture of the little girl in front of the flowered wallpaper, the exact little girl of my dreams."

Beth exhaled a big breath, closed her eyes briefly, and slowly shook her head. "I was afraid you were going to say that." Then after a pause, she said, "Let's see."

After handing her the photo, she studied it closely, put one hand over her mouth, and continued to slowly shake her head. Finally, she took a big breath and gave it back to me. "We're going to freaking-well figure this out, Sara. We will. I'm sure of it."

After putting the photo back in the envelope and passing her the diaries, I looked in her eyes and nodded slowly. "I really hope so." She reached over and gave my hand a squeeze.

Chapter Thirty

London | September, 2005

Day One

Our first full day in London was Saturday. Because Mom had no room in her tiny flat provided by the university, she had generously booked us a room at the Hilton at Hyde Park. We arrived there mid-morning. To adjust to the London time zone, we had a "no napping" plan, so after checking in, we changed our clothes, then went outside and across the street to Kensington Gardens. Although puddles told the story of an earlier rain, and a heavy slate sky hung over the park, the Londoners were out walking, biking, and jogging throughout the grounds.

Beth and I wandered past an old-style carousel which

was about to open for the day, and then we headed down a side path and around a pond. A large group of swans was conducting their morning ablutions at the far edge, a gaggle of Canada geese wandered along the grasses nearby, and here and there some whining, nervous seagulls skittered about.

Mom had arranged for the three of us to have lunch with a woman she referred to as Aunt Beatrice. Apparently she was not really related, but her mother and Great Grandma Sadie were close friends before GG moved to Canada, and over the years, Aunt Beatrice had kept in touch with Grandma and Grandpa. Mom had met with Aunt Beatrice a few times and described her as something of a London historian who might be helpful to us in some manner.

Aunt Beatrice had made a twelve noon reservation at The Old Bank of England, which apparently was a renovated bank-turned-pub. Mom met us at the hotel and handed us each a welcome present of umbrellas. We hugged and laughed, then she hailed an iconic black cab and we headed to the restaurant.

Mom had cautioned us that Beatrice "abhors tardiness," so we arrived a full twenty minutes early. Aunt Beatrice was already there. She was a stout, bustling, no-nonsense lady in her mid seventies, dressed in a knee length black skirt, a tweedy brown jacket, and a cream blouse which sported a flouncy bow. Thick-heeled shoes and rather gaudy patterned hose completed her ensemble. She clutched a large purse with both arms.

Aunt Beatrice nodded primly at Mom, and then in a

stage whisper, spoke to the hostess at the front of the restaurant. "My dear, please don't even think of seating us near the loo. And I will not abide air-conditioning blowing down the back of my neck."

When I glanced at my sister, she folded in her lips tightly, raised her eyebrows, and bugged out her eyes, which of course caused me to snicker, which then caused Mom to jab me in the ribs with her elbow. Beth quickly turned and gazed out the glass door to check the street activity, but I saw her shoulders shaking.

Eventually, we were settled at a table for four, and only then did Aunt Beatrice allow Mom to introduce Beth and I. Beatrice nodded formally to each of us, and immediately turned her attention to the place setting in front of her. First she lifted the water glass to the light, then studied the silverware, rejecting the knife which apparently displayed some kind of spot. She proceeded to berate our waitress for this transgression, who removed the knife in a flustered manner and quickly returned with a new knife and three menus.

With considerable tsk-tsking, Beatrice sharply informed her, "There are four of us here, as most people would deduce at a glance." The waitress mumbled an apology which included about three "ma'ams" and scurried off for the missing menu. I expected she was also pleading with her colleagues to take over our table.

Aunt Beatrice proceeded to provide us with a detailed overview of the available lunch possibilities, quickly ruling out some items and guiding us towards the best four choices. She clearly expected us to take her advice, and thinking of the poor waitress and the potential conse-quences of disobedience, we all complied. I drew the line at steak and kidney pie, but chose the Cornish pastry, a hand-held affair filled with beef and potato.

It was only after lunch was ordered and Beatrice had a small glass of sherry in front of her, that she turned her attention to us. She knew the general reason for our trip to London, but wanted the details. I focused on Great Grandma's diaries, explaining how they came to be in my possession, and briefly described GG's early life in London. Beatrice listened carefully while occasionally taking minuscule sips of sherry. She asked several short, to-the-point questions, which left me feeling like a student being quizzed by a teacher. Our lunch arrived promptly and we ate in silence for some time, until Beatrice laid down her fork and summarized what I had shared.

"So your great grandmother began writing these di-aries in 1910 when she started working at a boot factory. After about ten years, she emigrated to Canada, by herself. By that time her father had been committed to an insane asylum diagnosed with what was called Religious Mania. The diaries mention that Sadie's father had a younger sis-ter who disappeared when she was 3 or 4 years old, while she and the brother were out looking for food, perhaps at an apple orchard. And you want to find out what happened to this child who disappeared approximately 132 years ago."

The woman's listening skills were impressive, as was

her ability to get to the heart of the matter, her quick mental math, and the fact that she appeared to take this as a serious undertaking, not a fool-hardy mission. She finished up the last of her steak and kidney pie and pondered, while we all waited in silence.

"Do you have any other documents or personal items of your great grandmother's, besides the diaries?"

I told her about the shoe-making hammer and anvil, the certificates from the factory and the union, one of which indicated her address at the time, and the little Bible that she was given in 1908 by her Sunday School, for "Attendance and Good Conduct."

"Oh, well then, the Bible no doubt has the name of her church in it, correct?" Beth and I stared blankly at each other which caused Aunt Beatrice to huff in exasperation. "Young ladies, you will need to improve your observational skills if you expect to solve this or any other mystery. Did you bring the Bible with you?"

Thankfully, Mom jumped into the breach. "Sara can phone her grandparents and get them to take a look at the Bible."

Nodding thoughtfully, Beatrice pursed her lips. "In years gone by, churches kept records of all births, marriages, and deaths of the parishioners. When new people joined the church the pastor usually recorded the family details and what church they had previously attended. Back in your great grandmother's time, families often stayed in the same area for generations, so perhaps this child attended the same church as your great grandmother."

As I raised my eyebrows at Beth, she nodded, then Beatrice continued. "So even if the child never attended that particular church, the records may indicate what church her family, or your great grandmother's family, had previously attended. You may be able to find out when the child died, or went missing, or at the very least determine the year she was born. If the records are there," she added, "it will give you a pretty good idea of the area where she lived."

Beth and I exchanged excited, wide-eyed faces at each other, and it seemed she really wanted to do a high-five.

"That's amazing, Aunt Beatrice," I said. "We'll phone Grandma and Grandpa today and get as much information as possible."

"Alright, now ladies, tell me why you want to know what happened to this child. I believe there is something more to the story." She looked from Beth to me. "Am I right?"

Nodding slowly, I said, "You're right, Aunt Beatrice, there is more to the story." Then I launched into a summary of my dreams, the little ghost, my uncle's similar visions, the resident ghost at the Three Sisters' Inn, plus the weird details within previous generations of our family.

Aunt Beatrice listened intently and nodded several times. "So this child is not at peace. She needs to be found. She needs closure. What was the child's name?"

"We don't know her name," I said.

"Ah. Do you know the year your great great grandfather was born?"

I shook my head.

"The church records may have his date of death and of birth, and if the records are complete you should be able to find her name and the precise date of her death or disappearance." She paused, and added, "Then she will have to be appeased somehow."

Beth and I looked at each other and Beth raised her eyebrows slightly. "Aunt Beatrice, what do you mean by appeased?" she asked. "If we do find information about the child, we don't really know what should be done."

Aunt Bea looked thoughtfully at the cup of tea in her hand and nodded to herself. After a moment, she looked up and brightened. "You must come for tea on Thursday and tell me what you have learned. I have some ideas to explore and we can discuss it all then."

"That would be wonderful," I said. "Thank you so much for everything, Aunt Beatrice."

In front of the restaurant, our four umbrellas popped open against a considerable downpour, Aunt Bea hailed a cab while the three of us headed to a nearby tube station, as Mom had decided to introduce us to the London Underground. We trotted after her down steps from street level, expecting to board a train. But incredibly, we then descended further and further on a total of three long steep escalators. I was flabbergasted. When we unearthed like moles at Notting Hill Gate tube station, the unwavering crowds carried on as if rushing along at break-neck speeds so far below the earth's surface was perfectly normal.

Later that afternoon, Grandma and Grandpa clarified by phone that on the inside cover of Sadie's Bible was a handwritten note indicating, *St Ann's Church, Avenue Road, Tottenham*. The hotel concierge indicated it would take about an hour by car to drive there from our hotel. Mom had to work the next day, but kindly offered to hire us a car and driver.

Chapter Thirty-One

London | September, 2005

Day Two

At nine o'clock the following morning, Beth and I climbed into the back seat of the hired car. I indicated our destination as St. Ann's Church, and provided the address to the driver. The sky was dull, and spitting rain hit the windshield as we skirted along the edge of Regent Park and drove by the London Zoo. Our driver indicated the zoo had been first developed in the late 1800s.

"So it's the same zoo Great Grandma Sadie visited with her friends and sister," I said to Beth. "Amazing."

As we drove through an area called Camden, the sky started to lighten and the rain stopped. The driver had a

GPS and easily located St. Ann's. Just as the sun peeked through the clouds, we found ourselves standing in front of an amazingly beautiful little church.

Although a sign on the front door advised us to *Enter for Inquiries*, the door was locked, so we walked around the lawns admiring the lovely exterior and taking pictures. The church was built of vastly irregular sizes and shapes of pale brick, and to the right of the signed door was an arched doorway at the bottom of a square, three-story tower. The middle body of the church had three large arched windows, as well as six tiny higher arched windows just below the roof line, and beyond that section was a beautiful high circular stained-glass window. On the side lawn, a darkened cement pillar with metal lettering read: *In Memory Of The Men Who Went Forth From St. Ann's And Gave Their Lives For Their Country In The Great War 1914-1918.*

A high solid wooden fence blocked us from going entirely around the church, so we backtracked and walked along the opposite side. There we found a faded plaque on the wall which indicated the church was built in 1861, but then towards the back of the church we met up with the wooden fence again. It had a door standing wide open, with a sign which read, *Keep Door Locked at All Times*. Hmm. Beth and I looked at each other.

"It's the only way to see the back of the church," Beth said.

Proceeding through the door, we saw the back of the church which appeared to be half of an octagonal shape. Beth thought it formed the sanctuary. There was an arched window on each of the four faces, with flowering shrubs growing below and a narrow strip of grass between the shrubs and the neighbouring property behind. As we rounded the end of the sanctuary we were surprised to see a very pale older gentleman sitting at a patio table with a newspaper and a cup of tea. We were so close we could have reached out and shook hands.

The man looked up in surprise and I mumbled, "Oh sorry, we just wanted to see the back of the church." We kept moving.

We eventually came to the fence on the other side, and had to backtrack past the man again to get out. Beth felt the need to provide some kind of explanation. "Our Great Grandmother attended this church," she said to him. "And we've come from Canada to see it."

"Oh," he responded, "Well, let me know if you'd like to see inside."

Turned out he was the church Vicar, and although we expressed considerable enthusiasm about going inside the church, he rather pointedly said nothing more and went back to his newspaper. We went out the open gate, and returned to the side lawn.

Then Beth pointed to the building next door. "Look, it's St. Ann's Church Hall. Let's see if anyone is there." We wandered over, but to our disappointment, the building was locked and no one responded to the door buzzer.

As we turned back around, we noticed that a tall Black women in layers of bright draping clothing, had exited the building across the street and was marching toward us.

"Hello, hello," she called out. "I'm the caretaker and secretary for the church and the hall." As she reached us, she shook our hands with enthusiasm, and said, "I'm Celia... you wanted to see inside our lovely church?"

Apparently, the seemingly indifferent Vicar had phoned her. Celia presented as a friendly, chatty woman with a broad face, wide smiling mouth, dark expressive eyes, and seemed genuinely tickled when we told her that we were from Canada and that our great grandmother had attended the church.

"And we have her 1908 Bible from when she completed Sunday school here."

"That's amazing," said Celia as she unlocked the door and we went inside. "Now ladies," she explained with obvious pride, "our little church was built in the Gothic style of architecture which came back into style in the mid 18th century."

A high vaulted ceiling ran the length of the church, and about a third of the way in from each of the side walls stood an imposing line of massive cement archways which marched up to the sanctuary. The high miniature windows that we viewed from outside perched above these arches.

As we walked down the aisle, Celia pointed to the large, circular, stained-glass window. "That's called a rose window. Just take a look at the complex design. It's a real beauty. And look, the sun just came out. Gives it a magical glow, don't you think? Let me tell you, that doesn't happen very often in dreary old London. Must be a good omen for you two, I think."

It was a magnificent little church. For a few minutes we stood quietly and soaked it all in until Celia couldn't take the silence any longer and started asking questions. This led to a discussion about our hope of finding information about Great Grandma Sadie's parents.

"Apparently, there was a little girl who would have been Great Grandma's aunt, who disappeared and presumably died at a very young age," I explained to Celia. "She was never found. I'm not sure if it's even possible, but we would really like to figure out what happened to her."

"Oh, a mystery!" Celia exclaimed, "I love mysteries!"

We laughed and I asked, "So would there be any church records from around the 1860s to the 1920s?"

To our absolute amazement, Celia assured us there were. "Oh yes, my dears, the records go all the way back to 1861 when the church was built, and I'd love to help you look. I do have to get permission from Vicar Black to let you see them. Sometimes he can be a bit finicky, but let me call him."

She whipped out her cell phone and punched in numbers while she walked away from us and out the door. Beth and I gave each other "can you believe it?" looks, and I clamped my hand over my mouth to keep myself from whooping out loud. Then we snapped pictures from every angle in the church and eventually, Celia returned.

She grinned and shook her head at the same time. "He's a good man but very protective of his church," she said. "However, I convinced him there's no reason to keep all these ancient records if nobody ever looks at them! We actually just finished a massive organization of the records in preparation for them being sent to the London Metropolitan Archives next month. All the small churches are being encouraged to send records to the Archives, where I guess they can be better preserved. Anyway, a year ago it would have been a nightmare to find anything here, but now I think we have a pretty good shot at it."

"Celia, that's fantastic!" I exclaimed.

"The Vicar stipulates that I must be with you at all times, so it can't be today, as I have to finish this week's church bulletin and send it to the printers. I could help you tomorrow. Can you come back first thing in the morning?"

"We definitely can," Beth assured her.

Then Celia asked where we were staying and how we had travelled to the church. We confessed that our mother had treated us to the Hilton at Hyde Park, and had also hired a car and driver, which were waiting on the street.

Celia tsk-tsked several times. 'You can take the tube from Notting Hill Gate station near your hotel, and get off at the Tottenham East station, and it's only a three block walk here. Text me when you get on the train, and I'll meet you at the station at this end."

After thanking her profusely, we exchanged cell phone numbers and then headed out to find our car.

Chapter Thirty-Two

London | September, 2005
Day Three

True to her word, when we emerged from Tottenham station the next morning, our new best friend, Celia, stood on the street, waving and yohoo-ing to attract our attention (and everyone else's). She flowed towards us, with her long purple dress and multi-coloured scarves whipping around her in the breeze.

As we met on the sidewalk she said, "Okay girls, we've got us some work to do, so let's boogie." She headed off briskly, talking non-stop, with us hurrying to keep up.

When we arrived at the church, she took us down some side stairs and we entered a windowless, low-ceiling basement with rows of sturdy cardboard boxes on folding tables.

"The boxes are labelled in ten year spans," Celia explained. "We'll start with the year your great grandma was born, because if we find a record of her baptism, we'll likely find out the names of her parents."

After I supplied the information that Great Grandma was born on November 28, 1895, Celia grabbed a nearby folding chair, motioned for us to do the same, and we set up in front of the box labelled 1891-1901.

Celia pulled out latex gloves from her pocket and handed a set to each of us. "We need to wear these so we don't get oils or sweat on the paper." Then she lifted a slim book out of the box and opened it to the first thick, yellowed page which was titled *Baptisms* in swirly hand-writing.

"Entries are generally in chronological order from the date of baptism, but sometimes it was the date of birth that was entered instead, and sometimes nothing was entered in the book at all and you have to go through these piles of actual baptism certificates. Clearly the church secretaries a hundred and twenty years ago were not as organized as I am." She laughed.

She followed the threads of two gold bookmarks and showed us a page with the title, *Marriages*, and another titled *Deaths*. She cautioned us that each page and separate paper had to be carefully lifted, not flicked over from the corner. "And everything must be kept in the current order or both the Vicar and I will have your heads!"

Celia then set the book in front of Beth and I. "You

two can work on the book together," she said, "but in case the baptism was not recorded, I'll start looking at the actual certificates at the same time." We agreed this made sense and we all started at our jobs.

Then Celia added, "Back then, babies were usually baptized very quickly after birth because there was a pretty high chance of them dying in infancy. So start at her birthdate. And the pages are so delicate and the binding so worn you should only turn one page at a time."

Beth and I slowly and carefully made our way through the pages to the records for the end of November and then started studying the entries. We went all the way to the end of February with no luck, and although Celia said it would be unusual, she suggested we do one more month.

We were just unsuccessfully finishing the month of March, when Celia let out a whoop that made us both jump. "This is it!"

She set a faded but legible paper in front of us, with the title, *Certificate of Baptism, St. Ann's Church, Tottenham, England.*

Beth read out loud, "*In the name of God; Father, Son and Holy Spirit, this certifies that Sadie Elizabeth Hall, born in Tottenham England, the 28th day of November 1895, was received into the household of God by Holy Baptism on the 30th day of November 1895.*"

And there at the bottom of the page was what we are looking for. Beside the word *Parents*, was written Isaac and Hattie Hall.

Beth and I looked at each other and then at Celia who

had her elbow on the table and was resting her chin in her hand and grinning.

"Okay, so you didn't know the name of your great, great grandfather, but you do know the year of his death, right?" We affirmed this as being 1923. "So now, with his name, we can hopefully find his death notice which should provide his birth date and his parents' names. And that information should help to figure out something about Isaac's little sister."

It all sounded reasonable, so Celia retrieved the box that included 1923, and opened the appropriate book to the *Deaths* page. Beth and I started carefully making our way through the pages, while Celia went to make a photocopy of the baptism certificate.

Within twenty minutes we found the entry for Isaac's death, December 13, 1923 and we were amazed that yes, it indicated he was born on April 23rd, 1876 and that he was the son of Walter and Gertrude Hall.

Celia said, "I can't make a photocopy from the book as it would damage the fragile spine, so you have to write down the information."

I recorded the details and then looked at Celia. "Do we have another step?" I asked.

Celia was a thinker and after a minute she said, "We should try and determine whether Isaac was baptized in this church or not." She proceeded to find the Baptism box for 1871-1881 but an hour later we were disappointed to conclude that Isaac had not been baptized in that church.

But then Beth remembered something, "Aunt Beatrice

told us that sometimes the details of new church members were recorded when they first joined a church."

"Oh, that's right," said Celia thoughtfully. "Sometimes they were. So we'd have to look at all the years between when Isaac was born and when he died, to see if there is an indication of when the family moved here and what church they'd come from. She raised her eyebrows. "That is about forty-five years of records, ladies!" She paused. "But wait a minute, you said the sister who went missing was younger than him?" We affirmed. "And do you have any reason to believe there were other younger children in the family?"

We thought about this and yes, it seemed likely Isaac had more than one younger sibling.

"So then," Celia slowly continued, "let's start looking at the first few years after Isaac's birth. We can look in both the baptism records and the new members' records." She found the appropriate records and handed us the baptism book. "So you're looking for any child with the last name of Hall. And I'm looking for the family of Walter and Gertrude Hall joining the church. Unfortunately the records of new members back then were often pretty hit and miss, but it's worth a try."

For two hours the three of us slogged through the records from 1877 to 1882 and plodded onwards to 1883. Then Celia found it. Under *New Members* in 1883 it listed Gertrude Hall, wife of deceased Walter Hall, and it listed the children as Charlie, Isaac, Clarence, Bertha and Phyllis. But most importantly, it recorded the parish they came from as St. John Church, Vartry Road, Stamford Hill.

Celia seemed even more excited than Beth and I. "I know that church!" she exclaimed. "It's just a few miles from here." She decided to phone St. John right then, but there was no answer, so she left a message with a brief explanation of our request, and provided both her phone number and mine.

It was one-thirty in the afternoon and we had been at it since eight-thirty in the morning. We convinced Celia to let us buy her lunch, then tidied up and walked to a nearby restaurant.

After we each ordered a plate of fish and chips, Celia asked, "So how did you become interested in finding out about this child who went missing so long ago?" Beth and I exchanged looks, which Celia noticed and said, "What? What is it? I told you I loved mysteries."

So I launched into an abridged version of the entire saga, including my nightmares of Great Great Grandfather, (aka Raving Rasputin), and also the little girl ghost at the Three Sisters' Inn who seemed to be the same girl I saw and dreamt about in Canada. With rapt attention and brown eyes sparkling, Celia listened to the whole epistle.

"The little girl is definitely looking for closure," she proclaimed confidently. "She wants to be found, acknowledged, and properly buried, or at the very least properly acknowledged, and some type of ceremony performed for her." It seemed to me like an impossible mission, but I kept those feelings to myself.

By the end of lunch, Beth and Celia had decided we

should take a taxi to St. John Church, just in case we might find someone there. We were disappointed however, to find the church locked up and no one about. The skies were heavily drizzling by then, so with raised umbrellas, we walked around the building, which was more utilitarian and much less picturesque than St. Ann.

"This is ghastly," mumbled Celia. "No wonder they changed churches."

Beth and I laughed.

We all took a taxi to the tube station and promised to be in touch as soon as one of us heard from the St. John staff. Although we had learned quite a bit, I was feeling somewhat deflated, and asked Celia, "Do you really think we'll be able to find out something about Isaac's little sister?"

"Well, I think we have a good chance at it. Oh, I never asked you… do you know the little girl's name?"

"No, I wish we did."

"Okay, but we know the approximate year of her death," mused Celia. "We know her last name, and we know her parents' first and last names. So we should be able to find her in the records… well, if we're able to locate the records and if her birth was recorded."

"That's a couple of significant ifs," I lamented.

Chapter Thirty-Three

London | September, 2005
Day Four

By ten the next morning we had heard nothing, and both Beth and I were getting worried. Then at eleven o'clock, Celia called to report she had just talked to the church caretaker at St. John who would meet us that afternoon. We were ecstatic and asked Celia if she would like to join us.

"Oh, I'm definitely coming!" she said. "I'm hooked on this mystery now."

It was one-thirty when Beth and I arrived at the Tottenham station. We walked outside to lovely sunshine and the sound of yoo-hooing coming towards us in a long red and orange bohemian dress. Celia hugged us as though we had been best friends for years, flagged down a taxi, and we were on our way.

During the drive, my right knee jittered up and down and I chewed on the side of my thumb. Eventually, Beth gently took my hand away from my face and gave it a squeeze. I squeezed back and we kept holding hands until we got to the church a few minutes later.

The documents at St. John's were not nearly as well organized as those at St. Ann's, but after two hours of searching, the death records from 1880 through to 1883 were found. We figured Isaac's little sister probably would have died in that time frame. To our shock, on the first page of 1880 there was an entry for Daisy Hall, who died July 13, with parents listed as Walter and Gertrude Hall. Beth and I were excited until Celia pointed out the entry of Daisy's birth, which was July 8, 1880.

"She was only five days old!" Beth gasped and we stared at each other and then back at the page.

"As I told you, back then, many babies didn't live very long," Celia said. "Let's keep looking."

Under 1881, we found the death of Herbert Hall on September 10, with parents Walter and Gertrude Hall, and saw that his birth date was June of the same year. He died at three months of age.

"How could Gertrude stand it?" Beth muttered. "She was probably pregnant most of her married life… I wonder how many more she lost?"

"Well, let's see if she lost one more in 1882," said Celia, "…a girl born between '77 and '80."

As we all turned our eyes back to the book, a bird smashed into the window directly across the table from where we sat. I was so tightly wound that I jumped and actually screamed from the shock.

"Oh man," I said, holding both hands to my chest and tried to calm my breathing, "Sorry... but I'm really freaked out for some reason."

"Okay," said Beth. "Take a couple big breaths and let's just get through this."

We all turned our attention back to the book and started at the top of 1882 under *Deaths*. Beth slowly ran her finger down the page all the way to the bottom, then Celia carefully turned the page and Beth's finger went to the top entry.

"*Sara Hall,*" it read, "*Disappeared, Presumed Dead, September 27, 1882. Born June 21, 1879. Parents Walter and Gertrude Hall.*"

The page swam in front of me, and I couldn't catch my breath. Then everything went black and it felt like I dropped through the floor of the church and was plummeting through ice-cold blackness, spinning through time and space. Dimly, I heard Beth call my name, but her voice seemed very far away. Then Celia was shaking me, and abruptly I snapped back into the light, gasping for breath as if surfacing from underwater. Beth rubbed my back and Celia squeezed my hand in both of hers.

"Where did you go, girl?" Celia asked. "Because you surely left here."

I gulped big breaths of air that weirdly smelled of rusted metal.

Then Celia said, "Sara, your hands are ice cold and you're shivering. I'll go look in the lost and found for a jacket or something… people always leave stuff at churches, and then I'll figure out how to make you a cup of tea."

My vision was blurry, but I managed to find Beth's face. "We have the same name," I whispered. "All this time she's been saying her own name."

"Maybe that's why you have such a strong connection with her," Beth said. "When you saw her in the hallway last week, you thought she actually pondered your question about what you should do when you were here. Remember, you thought she was going to tell you something different? But she still just said 'Sara.'"

"Yes, but she said it differently. She whispered it, like it was a secret message, like she was trying to tell me something more. It's never been my name she was saying. It's her name. To solve the whole puzzle we have to find Sara."

We had supper with Mom that night and updated her on our discoveries. Beth told her about me blacking out.

"Sara, remember the day you skyped with Molly from the Three Sisters' Inn?" Mom asked. "You blacked out or something then. Was today like that?"

"Well, yes, but today was more intense. I actually felt like I was underwater and couldn't breathe."

Mom shook her head and rubbed my shoulder.

"When you skyped with Molly that day," Beth said, "you found out that your little ghost is the same little ghost as at the inn. And today we determined her birth and death dates, and that you have the same name. So these falling-type incidents occurred both times you uncovered an important piece of information about her."

We all nodded.

By the end of the meal, Beth decided the next step should be a tour of the Three Sisters' Inn.

"Oh," Mom said. "Molly already knows you're here and that you'll want to see the place. She was fine with you visiting either tomorrow or the next day. I have her cell phone number and will try to confirm a meeting for tomorrow morning."

Later that night, when my sister and I were in our beds and the lights were out, the events of the day reeled through my mind. "Beth, when I had my incident today, did I scream?"

"No, you didn't... why?"

"Well, in that whirling blackness, I heard someone scream... I just wondered if it was me."

Later that evening, I skyped with Jesse and updated him on the day's events. He was actually speechless for a moment when I told him the little girl's name was Sara, and that all along she had been saying her own name.

As always, Jesse wanted details and asked several specific questions. "I've been pondering something," he said. "And it might not mean anything, but this is what I'm wondering. There seems to be a lot of repeated imagery about being or going down into the earth, and I'm wondering if that has something to do with the little girl's disappearance."

He explained that he started thinking of this possibility because two 11-year old boys disappeared a couple days before in cottage country in Ontario, and were found twenty-four hours later down the shaft of an old mine. Fortunately, they sustained only minor injuries, but it made him think about my great aunt disappearing as a child.

"So, think about it, Sara. Your coffin dream involves an underground image, although I started wondering if it could be something other than a coffin… in the dream do you ever actually have a look at what you are confined in?"

"Well, I never actually *see* a coffin in the dream, no. I just feel the confinement around me. So maybe it could be something else."

Jesse continued, "And both times, when you took a big step closer to identifying little Sara, you had the sensation of dropping down through a dark tunnel or hole, right? Both today and during the Skype?"

"That's true…" I paused. "And maybe there's one more thing. Remember the time I saw Sara out my bedroom window, and she was down on the lawn?"

"Yeah, that was only a couple weeks ago, right?"

"Yes. Maybe I didn't tell you, but when she disappeared that time she looked like she vanished straight down into the ground."

"Interesting. So here's what I'm thinking. When you

go to the Three Sisters' Inn, you should query about any kind of holes in the ground, could be old mine shafts, wells, caves, maybe some kind of underground bunker? Can you think of anything else?"

I said I would share his theory with Mom and Beth, and we would ponder it on our way to the Three Sisters' Inn.

Chapter Thirty-Four

London | September, 2005

Day Five

At eight fifteen the next morning, Mom, Beth, and I were in a taxi. The sun was actually shining for once, which we took as a good omen. When we arrived at the Three Sisters' Inn, we were greeted enthusiastically by Molly. She was accompanied by a tall, slim older gentleman with pale skin, a full white beard and moustache, and matching bushy white eyebrows that framed the top of his dark rimmed glasses. Behind the glasses were intense blue eyes.

"This is Mr. Cooper," Molly explained. "He lives nearby and comes to visit us on a regular basis. I thought he would be a good person for you to talk to because he actually helped build the Three Sisters' Inn."

"That's amazing," I said. "Thanks so much for coming to meet us."

As we introduced ourselves, Mr. Cooper grinned and shook hands all around. "Miss Molly here tells me you're interested in our resident ghost. I saw the wee mite a few times when we were building the place, and a couple times since."

This really piqued our interest, and Beth and I started asking questions at the same time. Mr. Cooper laughed and Molly suggested we all sit down for "a cuppa" while we heard Mr. Cooper's story, and then we would go for a tour. I passed on the tea, but while the others sipped, we learned that Mr. Cooper was a young man of 20 in 1950, when he helped to build the inn.

"That was just five years after the end of the war," Mr. Cooper said. "The original Three Sisters' Pub was damaged in the bombing and the main part had been repaired, but it was really just a temporary solution. The owners, Mr. and Mrs. Harris, decided to build a bigger place that would also have rooms for overnight guests. They owned about three acres, so there was enough room to keep the pub running while the new place was being built. That plaza next door with the Tesco Convenience store is where the old pub used to be."

"Mr. Cooper," Beth said, "does the little ghost you saw when you built this place look the same as the ghost that has been seen recently?"

"Oh yes, it's the same little mite. I could never understand why she haunted a brand new building. There were other buildings in the city with a ghost back then, well, there still are… but there's generally a story that goes with each one. The person died tragically in the house or something along that line."

When everyone had finished their cuppa, Molly and Mr. Cooper led the way up the stairs to the second floor of the inn, where Molly unlocked doors to three of the eight bedrooms, the others being occupied. I kept an eye out for little Sara, but she did not reveal herself. The rooms were comfortable and cozy looking, with floral printed bedspreads and a tolerable amount of ruffles.

The last room we visited went overboard with floral wallpaper as well as a floral bedspread, which I found a bit dizzying. Then just before we left the room, I clenched Beth's arm and hissed, "The wallpaper!"

She raised her eyebrows, studied the large pink and mauve flowers on the walls, and then her eyes flew open wide. She nodded slowly and we stared at each other in silence. It was the wallpaper from the photo on my cell phone. The little girl's photo originated in this very room.

Beth and I were a bit shaky going back down the stairs, but we pulled ourselves together and followed the tour through the formal dining room and into the kitchen where staff were already working on lunch preparations. We exited through French doors onto a lovely attached patio, then down a few steps to the lawn and walked towards the separate terrace.

The terrace was the area in which Mom and her friend

had lunch when Molly first told her about the inn's resident ghost. A warm breeze rustled the leaves of two gnarly old apple trees which had a few red apples still clinging to their branches. Birds flitted busily about. Molly informed us proudly that apple crisp was a standard on the menu every fall, made of apples from these two ancient trees.

"Most of the apples have been picked already," Molly said. "We can't have them bonging down on our patron's noggins, can we?!" She hooted out a laugh which caused us all to join in.

Mr. Cooper chuckled and said, "I'm a regular customer for that apple crisp every year... just had some last week. Best apple crisp in the country if you ask me." And he smacked his lips for emphasis.

"Well, we should probably have some of that before we leave," I said. "So, Mr. Cooper, we have the idea that the little girl might have fallen into some kind of hole or opening and died there. Are you aware of any shafts or holes into the ground on or near the property?"

Mr. Cooper looked at me and one bushy white eyebrow rose up high, as if pulled by an invisible string from above.

"Well, that would explain things," he said, seemingly to himself.

As I asked what he meant, he started walking back towards the inn at a fair clip, muttering "That would explain it... that makes sense."

We all followed him, with Mom, Beth, and I exchanging puzzled glances.

"Molly," said Mr. Cooper as we crossed the patio, "we need to go into the basement. See if you can find Lucas, would you?"

Molly explained to us that Lucas was the owner/manager, and she hustled off, but quickly returned accompanied by a striking middle-aged man, who had mocha coloured skin, dark hair and eyes, and a ready smile. He wore black pants and a crisp white dress shirt with sleeves meticulously rolled up half-way to his elbows. In one hand he carried a large set of keys. He greeted Mr. Cooper warmly, and Molly introduced the rest of us to Mr. Lucas Garcia.

"I understand our little ghost might be two-timing us?" he said. "Visiting you in Canada, of all places?"

We acknowledged this and then Mr. Cooper spoke up. "Lucas, I'm sorry to be a nuisance, but I need to take them into the wine cellar. Sara here has just made me think of something that might be very relevant."

"It is no problem at all, Mr. Cooper," Mr. Garcia said with a smile. He led us to a hallway just off the kitchen which ended at a basement door and paused to caution us that the steps beyond were narrow and steep.

Just before I took my first step down, a cold gust of wind hit me in the face. I gasped and stepped back in surprise, bumping into Beth. "Did you feel that?" I asked her.

"Feel what?" She looked me in the eyes and shook her head.

Biting my lower lip, I headed down the stairs with Beth's hand on my shoulder. At the bottom, we looked around and saw shelves of canned goods and bins with labels for Christmas decorations, light bulbs, and extension cords.

Mr. Cooper asked the manager, "So Lucas, if you don't mind, I'd like to show them the in-ground wine cooler." The manager nodded, unlocked a nearby door, and flicked a light switch. I braced myself as I went through the door, and sure enough, a cold blast of air hit my face hard enough to blow back my hair. With wide eyes, Beth took my hand.

We were in a medium-sized room lined with shelves filled with resting bottles of wine. Mr. Cooper walked over to the far wall, and with my heart picking up speed, I followed close behind, holding tightly to my sister's hand. There were several steps going down steeply into the ground. The walls of the opening were stone-lined and held narrow shelves filled with bottles of white wine.

Mr. Cooper gestured downwards, "This is the top section of a very old well. We didn't even realize it was here until after the foundation was dug. It was Mrs. Harris who said the top part should be used as a natural cooler for white wine. So we crisscrossed the opening down there with rebar and laid a floor over top. I did most of the stone work myself, covering over the old dirt walls. Then we put in those shelves, and it's been used as a wine cooler ever since."

My vision had started to swirl and I abruptly went down on my knees, then leaned forward a bit, as if getting a better view. Immediately, Beth settled down beside me and I clutched her hand like a life-line, while bracing against the sensation of tumbling forward into a black hole. Her presence grounded me and verified that I was, in fact, still sitting at the top of the shaft.

Beth loudly asked, "How deep would the old well have been, Mr. Cooper? And how old do you think it was?"

Part of my mind registered that her volume was for me, not Mr. Cooper. Gradually the darkness started to recede and I tried to focus on Mr. Cooper's reply.

"Well, this part is twelve feet deep, and with flashlights we could see down about another twelve feet, I would say. It got quite narrow at the bottom so it was hard to see how far it actually went. And of course, the top eight feet or so had already been cut off when the foundation was dug. The well seemed to have pre-dated the old house that was further down the property and had been transformed into the original pub. Anyway, it was a very old well when we found it over fifty years ago. You said the little girl disappeared in 1882. I would guess this well was already old and probably unused by that time."

"So the little girl may have fallen into the well and the searchers couldn't find her," Beth suggested.

"Sure, she could have. This area may have been mainly apple orchards at that time, but it wouldn't have been the pristine, cleared setting of orchards today. It would have been over-run with wild growth which could easily have covered the top of an old hand-dug well." Mr. Cooper petted his beard thoughtfully. "A ghost was haunting a brand new building, I just never could figure that out. But if she died in the well, and we built the inn over top, then it all makes sense."

Yes, I guess it did all make sense. I looked at Beth, then gazed back down the stairs.

"You okay?" she whispered. I nodded yes, and with a final squeeze to my hand, she stood up. "Mr. Garcia," she said, "I'm not sure how much Molly has told you about our interest in your resident ghost." With his encouragement, she launched into a succinct summary of our quest, and how we came to be at the Three Sisters' Inn.

Mr. Garcia stood with his left arm across his chest, and his right elbow resting on it. His forearm extended upwards, and he rested his chin on the heel of his hand. His index finger tapped thoughtfully against his lips as he listened carefully to Beth's monologue.

When she finished, he simply said, "Remarkable. Absolutely remarkable."

Then I stood up, and after a big breath to clear my head, took over from Beth. "So Mr. Garcia, I know it's a great deal to ask, but the only way to bring peace to our Great Great Aunt Sara and to our family, is to find out if she is down there, and if so, to give her a proper burial."

Mom added, "We would pay for the work, of course, and for any repairs to your premises."

Mr. Garcia stepped over to gaze down the hole and lightly clapped Mr. Cooper on the back. "It is quite the remarkable story, yes?"

"It surely is," Mr. Cooper agreed. "What are you going to do about it?"

"Well, the first thing I have to do is confer with my wife… that should always be the first thing, shouldn't it, ladies?"

We all laughed and then he suggested we go up to the pub where he would join us after he phoned his wife.

Twenty minutes later, we were enjoying the first sips of frosty beer when Mr. Garcia arrived. "My wife would like to meet you all and hear the whole story. She thinks she could be here in about an hour, would you mind staying that long?"

We assured him we would gladly have some lunch and wait for her. A little over an hour later, we had finished our plates of fish and chips and were savouring warm, yummy apple crisp, when Mr. Garcia and his wife walked into the restaurant. The staff hustled to bring them each a chair and a beer and they joined us at our table.

Mrs. Garcia was a beautiful woman with mocha skin that matched her husband's, and mounds of black hair piled on her head. She wore large gold hoop earrings and bright red lipstick, and was very excited to hear all the details of our story.

As soon as we finished retelling our tale, Mrs. Garcia looked at her husband. "Well, we can't just leave the poor child down there, Lucas!" she exclaimed emphatically.

"You are right, of course you are right." He nodded thoughtfully, then turned back to us. "I will make some phone calls. I know of some people who may understand how to approach such a project. I will let you know as soon as I have gathered some information."

After we excitedly prattled our appreciation, Mom, Beth, and I headed back to the hotel. Later we had dinner sent up to the room and while eating chicken caesar salads, started wondering what we would do if we actually found little Sara's remains.

"Remember our tea date with Aunt Beatrice is tomorrow," Mom said. "I'm thinking she'll have some ideas for us."

This reminded me that I needed to update Celia or she would have our heads, so I punched in her number and put her on speaker phone. After we summarized our day, she responded with predictable enthusiasm.

"That is ab-sol-lute-ly amazing!" she shrieked. "Sara, did you have any weird reaction to the place... like you did in the church?"

After I described my reactions, Celia said emphatically, "It has to be the place where she died. It just has to be. You will tell me as soon as you know anything, right? Like, I even just want to know what the plan is, okay?"

"You'll be the first to know the plan, after we know the plan," I assured her.

At that moment, I couldn't even imagine what the plan might be.

Chapter Thirty-Five

London | September, 2005
Day Six

o our surprise, Mr. Garcia phoned at eleven the next morning, indicating he had formulated a plan, found people to carry it out, and asked us to return for one o'clock the next afternoon. We could hardly believe it. After a quick lunch, we got ready to go to Aunt Beatrice's for tea.

Mom arrived at the hotel at one-thirty so we could make our way to Aunt Beatrice's place together. (We assumed that she assumed we would get lost and/or be late if left to our own devices).

"Now Sara," Mom cautioned, "remember you must drink Aunt Beatrice's tea the way it is poured. She would be extremely offended if you didn't drink it, or if you watered it down… or if you grimaced."

I grimaced. The idea of drinking steeped, bitter tea put my teeth on edge just thinking about it.

Beth chimed in, "Mom's right, Sara. You can't run to the kitchen and water down your tea from the kettle. Aunt Bea would be horrified."

"Add some milk and lots of sugar," Mom suggested.

"Okay, okay, I'll handle it."

Mom had one further caution. "And no faces behind her back, you might get caught. Plus, you'll make your sister laugh." Beth and I both laughed and promised to be on our best behaviour.

Under cloudy but dry skies, we walked to the tube station, buying a bouquet of flowers en route. After a few minutes walking at the other end, we arrived at a large Victorian house which had been divided into three apartments—or rather, flats. Aunt Bea answered the door so quickly it was clear she had been waiting on the other side.

"Good, good, you're here on time," she said in a rush. "Lovely flowers, thank you very much. Now the loo is upstairs, first door on the right, so go on up and wash your hands for tea."

After following her instructions, Aunt Bea settled us into a small dining room, occupied by a dark, ornate, wooden table topped by a mauve tablecloth with lace edging. There was a matching sideboard far too large for the room, upon which stood a crystal vase already filled with our flowers. We man-handled the huge antique chairs and sat down.

Aunt Beatrice immediately took a knitted purple cozy off a waiting teapot on the sideboard and made her way around the table, pouring tea so strong I could smell the bitterness. I avoided making eye contact with Beth. We were encouraged to help ourselves to sugar and cream, so I shovelled three big spoonfuls of sugar into my tea, and poured in a touch of cream. There was a three-tiered china stand on the table with tiny, crustless sandwiches on the bottom plate, little biscuits on the middle plate, and sweets on the top level. Thankfully, Aunt Beatrice moved the stand towards Mom first, who took two sandwiches from the bottom shelf, and then Beth and I followed suit. I ate the most suspicious-looking sandwich first. The filling was orange and kind of sweet and gooey, and after eating it, I still had no idea what it was. The second one was crab and cucumber which suited me much better.

Halfway through the sandwich course, Aunt Beatrice set down her teacup, folded her hands in front of her on the table, and asked, "Well, tell me what you have found out about the little lost ghost."

We embarked on summarizing our activities over the last five days. We told her about our search through records at both churches, about Celia, and all about the Three Sisters' Inn.

"And now," I concluded, "the owner of the inn has

some kind of plan that we really know nothing about, but we are going to be there at one o'clock tomorrow and see what happens."

Aunt Bea looked at me and raised both eyebrows. "Well, well, I must say, I am quite favourably impressed with your progress. But do you think the owner of the inn is really going to dig up his wine cellar? And what will you do if, in fact, human bones are actually found down there?"

"Yes, I do really think that Mr. Garcia is going to dig up his wine cellar because he said he had a forensic anthropologist lined up to analyze any bones that might be found."

Aunt Beatrice nodded. "Excellent, excellent. So if the child is found, she will need a proper church service and a proper burial... would that Vicar from the church conduct the service, do you think?"

"We talked about that last night. I'm going to ask Celia whether she thinks the Vicar would do some kind of service."

"I suggest you make that contact as soon as possible," Aunt Bea encouraged, "to give the Vicar time to get his head around the idea. And is there anything else you are thinking of doing, to help the child move on?"

After I directed a blank look towards Beth she said, "Well, I kind of wondered if there was something else we should do, but I don't know what. Do you have any ideas, Aunt Beatrice?"

Aunt Bea pursed her lips in a meaningful manner.

"Well, I know a woman who used a psychic medium in her home once, to clear out a spirit who seemed unable to move on to the next realm. I actually phoned her yesterday and obtained the contact information for the psychic medium, whose name is Charlotte, and I spoke to her yesterday as well. After explaining the pertinent details of the situation, I inquired if her services might be available, should you want them. She was very agreeable and seemed relatively confident she could help the child move on into the next realm."

A little tingle zipped up my spine. Taking a big breath, I nodded and said, "Okay, if you think she could help, let's do it."

"Excellent. I will let her know."

We turned our attention back to the food. Apparently, the little items on the second tier of the fancy plate were scones. (Thankfully I had not used the term "biscuits" out loud.) We slathered them with strawberry jam, and added a dollop of something called clotted cream, which seemed rather like sloppy butter with a nutty, rich taste. Quite delicious, but the fat content was clearly off the scale.

Two hours later, we waddled our stuffed selves towards the tube station. Although the sun had come out, there was still a significant contingency of clouds in the sky.

As we waited on the platform, I phoned Celia. "Do you think the Vicar would perform a small service at the church and conduct a proper burial for Sara… if we find her?"

"I surely can convince him of that," she responded. "Leave it to me."

As soon as I turned off my phone, Mom said, "Sara, in preparation for your visit, I conducted an investigation into sunset viewing spots in London. Although predicting the sun's continued presence is always a risky business here, I think we should give it a try today. We could go for a walk along the Thames River down near the Tower of London, and if the skies are cooperative, we should have a great view of the sunset with the Tower Bridge in front."

"Mom, that's a fabulous idea!" I exclaimed, and Beth nodded enthusiastically in agreement.

The skies were amazingly cooperative. As the sun retreated, a rich scarlet dominated the high sky which faded to a purple-grey below. Muted blues and yellows lingered close to the horizon. The dark silhouette of the iconic bridge in the foreground presented a striking contrast to the spectacular pigments behind. It was an invigorating spectacle. As the colours faded, and the three of us linked elbows and strolled away, I somehow felt fortified for the following day's unknown events.

Chapter Thirty-Six

London | September, 2005
Day Seven

The next morning was bright and sunny, and Beth insisted we go on a two-hour walking tour called Hidden London. Our guide was excellent and took us through a labyrinth of tiny lanes around Fleet Street and along the Thames River, with bricked row housing that was over two hundred years old. The minuscule units had become fashionable and pricey, but originally, it was a very low-class area since the Thames River was basically an open sewer, responsible for a variety of illnesses including cholera. In the mid 1800s a proper sewage system was completed, and one hundred and fifty years later, the area had become a high-class yuppie neighbourhood. We also saw two small ancient churches, and a closed underground tube station that had been used as a bomb shelter during WWII, and had also housed British Museum artifacts for safe keeping.

As we walked along uneven cobbled streets the guide had us imagine ragged children running about, perhaps playing a game of Ring Around the Rosie. He claimed the nursery rhyme was actually about the Black Plague in the mid 1600s. The sneezing and rosy rash described in the rhyme were symptoms of the disease, and the "*pocket full of posies*" referred to herbs carried as protection and to mask the smell. The ending phrase of "*all fall down*" signified the death of the victims. Lovely.

As previously arranged, Mom met us at the end of the tour. While we had a quick lunch, the skies turned dark and foreboding, and during the cab trip to the Three Sisters' Inn, rain bucketed down. Upon our wet arrival, Molly immediately escorted us downstairs where we found Mr. and Mrs. Garcia, along with Mr. Cooper, talking to a young man and woman who were introduced to us as Evan and Lorrie. Their roles in the investigation were not provided. Wine bottles from the actual well had been packed into boxes and moved to the main part of the basement, while the wine shelving in the upper part of the room had been carefully sealed off with heavy plastic and plywood.

Mr. Garcia explained, "We have workmen coming to take out the old flooring that Mr. Cooper installed a few decades ago. So sorry to ruin your hard work, Peter." He smiled at Mr. Cooper. "Then Lorrie and Evan here will try to determine what is down there."

A few minutes later, a policeman arrived, apparently to witness the excavation, and then two middle-aged men came in, lugging additional equipment. The little room was congested as we all crowded around to watch the action.

The men set up a winch which was secured to a support post in the middle of the room. For added stability, the four heaviest observers were commandeered to stand on each corner of the winch platform. One of the workmen attached a harness to himself, clipped it onto the winch cable, and with a serious-looking saw in one hand, carefully descended the steep stairs. I took a deep breath and started methodically biting my fingernails.

Two hours later, the flooring, the steps, and the workman had been successfully removed from the hole, and Evan and Lorrie took over. The first thing they did was assemble a tripod over the well opening. The tripod appeared to have three separate small winches and they immediately attached a bright trouble-light to one and slowly lowered it into the hole. The winch measured off twenty-one feet when the light hit bottom.

Lorrie was busy and explained to the spectators, "I have here a special camera called a GoPro, which I'll attach to this second winch." Then she pointed to Evan who had a laptop set up on a small folding table. "Whatever is down there, we'll be able to see it on the laptop."

As the camera was slowly lowered into the well, both

my breathing and heart rate revved up, and I started chewing along the side of my thumbnail. We watched in suspense as the stone walls floated by on the laptop screen. When the camera reached the bottom, I held my breath and studied the screen nervously, butterflies swirling in my stomach. But there was nothing to see except stones, lumps of earth, and a couple chunks of rebar which had fallen down from above.

Before I could formulate my disappointment into a coherent thought, Mr. Cooper said, "So you're planning to move some of that debris, right?"

"Yes sir, we sure are," said Lorrie, and I started to breathe again.

Lorrie pulled up the camera and the light, attached pincers to the third winch, and lowered them into the well. When it reached the bottom, she lowered both of the other winches again to get a view of what was going on. Using a remote control to operate the pincers, she started bringing up chunks of dirt and stone which were dumped into heavy rubber tubs. It was a painfully slow process, and two hours later I had pretty much decided the whole operation was a bust.

Then, just before six o'clock, Owen said, "There, that could be a bone."

We all studied the laptop screen, which showed a small whitish something, mostly covered with dirt. Lorrie made minute adjustments, and the clamp dug into the area.

I clutched Beth's arm and stopped breathing again. In fact, the very room seemed to hold its breath as the pincers ascended the well. The apparatus arrived at the surface, slowly pivoted, and then opened its jaws into an empty tub. We couldn't see what had been deposited, but when Lorrie put on latex gloves from her back pocket, I knew there must be something.

I was unprepared for what she held up. It was a small human skull. There was gasping and murmuring around the room, and I braced myself for blackness and the falling sensation, but to my surprise, nothing like that happened. In fact, I felt a bit numb… and what was that other feeling that lurked inside me? Oh, it was relief. I felt relieved.

The policeman contacted the forensic anthropologist, who was on call if we needed her services, and then for the next two hours Lorrie and Evan continued the digging process and successfully retrieved several other bone pieces. When Dr. Jackson arrived, she confirmed that the remains were from a young child. There were not many teeth left in the jawbone but she thought the child would have been 3 or 4 years old—but I already knew that.

Dr. Jackson seemed extremely interested in the find. "I'll work on further analysis this evening and tomorrow," she said. She had clearly been apprised of our story previously, and looking at me said. "Sara, would you like to know if her DNA matches yours?"

A brief weakness washed over me, but fortunately Beth and Mom were holding me from both sides. I locked eyes with Dr. Jackson and nodded. Before we left, I spat into a test tube and left it with her.

The three of us, plus Mr. Cooper and Molly, wearily

headed to the pub for a late supper. After we ordered, I phoned Celia and filled her in. Her screech of excitement could be heard by everyone at the table and almost blew out my eardrum.

"And the Vicar has agreed to a small private service," she exclaimed. "I'll give him an update."

After a subdued supper and a return trip to our hotel, we convinced Mom to stay with us for the night. Beth and I collapsed into one bed, and Mom fell into the other.

Chapter Thirty-Seven

London | September, 2005
Day Eight

After breakfast, Mom headed back to her flat, and Beth said we needed a distraction while waiting to hear from the forensic-anthropologist. We decided to walk over to the Albert Memorial, about a thirty-minute stroll through Kensington Park.

Remarkably, the sky was bright blue with shifting clouds scattered throughout, and the outdoor exercise soothed my nervous tension. After we walked almost the width of the park, a sign directed us to the left, and we caught glimpses through the large trees of what looked like the top of an ornate church.

When we came into a clearing, we realized what we had seen was the top of the massive monument. A huge gold statue of Prince Albert sat under a gigantic canopy, ending in a towering steeple with rows of angels, and topped with a cross. Beyond each corner of the monument, down an abundance of steps, stood gigantic sculptures depicting the four continents over which Britain had influence during the Victorian era. Each was comprised of an enormous animal—elephant, camel, buffalo, ox—with several people gathered around. When Albert died at 42, a heart-broken Queen Victoria mourned for forty years. It was such a sad story, but the resulting monument was magnificent.

Realizing we were not far from Harrods, we walked another fifteen minutes to spend an hour gazing at purses that were worth more than my car, and wandering through the food courts. We purchased Stilton cheese for Grandma and Grandpa, a couple tins of Harrods' cookies for the boys, and take-out sandwiches for our lunch.

As we walked back across the park, munching on our sandwiches, Dr. Jackson phoned. We sat on a nearby bench and I put the phone on speaker.

"I have confirmed that the unearthed bones are from a female child of 3 or 4 years of age, and that she would have died between one hundred to one hundred and thirty years ago."

"That is amazing, Dr. Jackson," Beth said.

"Vitamin and mineral deficiencies leave clear markers in bone, so it is apparent that the child was suffering from rickets, a vitamin D deficiency," she continued. "Not all that unusual in those times. Now, the best place to look for DNA in very old remains is in the teeth, since enamel is the hardest substance in the body and protects the dentine within them, which contains the DNA. So Sara, I have been able to identify that your DNA and the little girl's DNA have a similar, distinctive pattern that proves you are related."

But I already knew that.

We contacted Mom who said she would inform Aunt Bea, and then we decided to consult with Celia. "Oh my," she said, after learning of the forensic results. "You were right all along. The mystery is solved. That's bloody amazing!"

"Celia, the forensic doctor needs to send the remains to a funeral home. So we were hoping you could help us out with that."

"Of course, of course… Hopewell Funeral Home is near the church. I'll give them a heads-up right now, and I'll inform Vicar Black too." She provided the contact information for Hopewell's and added, "Wait until I text you that I've spoken to the staff."

Before long we had a meeting set for later that afternoon at the funeral home. We let Celia know and she phoned us back. "Hopewell's is only five blocks from the Tottenham tube station. I'll meet you at the station and be your guide." Good old Celia.

Two hours later, we wandered out of Tottenham station

to the familiar sound of "yoohoo-ing" coming our way. Celia hugged us both fiercely and we started walking. At the funeral home, we signed papers allowing them to pick up Sara's remains from the forensic lab. Then the funeral director asked whether we wanted to cremate the remains and have an urn, or use a casket for the remains.

"Oh, we definitely want a casket," I said, and Beth nodded in agreement. Looking through a binder with pictures of caskets, we decided it should be plain and simple, more like the way caskets would have been at the time she died. We were told the bones could be wrapped in silk or satin, and we picked satin because it seemed to have a cozier, more comforting feel to it.

"Can it be pink satin?" Beth asked, and it could.

When we finished with the arrangements, I felt dissatisfied. "It doesn't seem like enough somehow," I said.

Celia (of course) came to the rescue. "You know, little Sara probably never ever had a doll," she said. "You could put a doll in there with her."

Beth and I both perked up. "Could we?" I asked the director, who indicated we could pretty much put whatever we wanted into the casket.

"So let's give her a teddy bear too," Beth blurted out.

I nodded, and could see the tears in my eyes reflected in her own. "Yes, we'll get her a teddy bear and a doll," I said and pressed my lips together while Beth sniffed and squeezed my hand.

Celia rubbed my back and nodded. "That's good, that's very good."

She had made arrangements with Vicar Black for a two o'clock service the next afternoon, and the funeral director assured us the preparations would be done and the casket moved to the church by noon the next day.

Celia, Beth, and I linked arms during our solemn walk back to the tube station, and Celia assured us she would meet the casket when it arrived at the church in the morning.

When Beth and I emerged from the tube station near our hotel, we immediately walked back through Kensington Park to Harrods. We muddled through rooms crowded with dolls and teddy bears, until we were satisfied we had found the perfect pair. Not too big, because Sara was just a little girl, and they were soft and snuggly and comforting—for little Sara and for us it seemed, as while standing in the checkout line we both cuddled and fussed with our purchases.

The line was slow-moving, and eventually Beth asked, "Would it be weird…" she hesitated and looked at me, "… would it be weird if we bought two of each of these and kept one for ourselves, as a sort of keepsake of little Sara?"

"I love that idea!" I said, so we charged off in search of a duplicate doll and teddy bear. With staff assistance, we were eventually successful, and after waiting in the checkout line again, we headed back to our hotel.

Chapter Thirty-Eight

London | September, 2005
Day Nine

At one-thirty the next day, Mom, Beth, and I arrived at St. Ann's to find Aunt Beatrice outside talking to Celia. To my surprise, another car soon pulled up, and out climbed Molly, Mr. Cooper, and Mr. and Mrs. Garcia, who were all there to say goodbye to the sad little ghost.

As prearranged, the casket lid was open with the small bones inside wrapped in satin. After everyone was seated, the Vicar nodded to us, and Beth and I walked to the front and laid the teddy bear and the doll inside the casket. He gently closed the lid and we sat back down. Unknown to everyone except Beth, I had also put in the photo of little Sara.

After a lovely, thoughtful service, I stayed behind in the church to have a few minutes alone. I laid my hands on top of the tiny coffin and said, "Sara, I am your great, great, grand-niece, and my name is Sara too, but I guess you know all that. I am very sorry that your life was terribly short and terribly difficult, and that you died such a horrible death all alone. And I'm so sorry that it took four generations for our family to find you. But we did find you, and I promise to come visit your grave every time I'm in England, for the rest of my life."

A tear dropped onto the coffin lid and I kissed my finger and planted it on top of my tear. "Go in peace, Sara. Go in peace, little girl."

In two cars, we followed the hearse to the nearby cemetery. The sky was overcast and moody and a fine mist dampened the air. Mom had brought a large bouquet of daisies and we gave one flower to each of the wonderful people who cared enough to come to the funeral of a little girl who died one hundred and twenty-three years ago. The tiny casket was lowered into the grave, and we each dropped a daisy on top. My vision was blurred as I walked away from the grave, arm in arm with my sister and mom.

At dusk we went back. It was a calm, dry evening, and my eyes wandered skyward where remnants of hazy purples intermingled with grey shifting clouds. Aunt Beatrice had arranged for the psychic medium to meet us at the cemetery and perform an additional ceremony, and we had collected both Aunt Bea and Celia en route. Charlotte, the psychic medium, was already at the gate when we arrived, and followed us in her car to the burial site, where the casket had already been covered with earth. Charlotte brought a box of small hurricane lamps with candles, which she lit and instructed us to place around the gravesite. Then we all stood on one side of the grave, holding hands, while Charlotte stood across from us and held a large bell in one hand.

"Little Sara," she said softly. "Sara? You have been trapped for such a long time, and I know you must be frightened, but we are here to help you. You are an Earthbound Spirit, but you need to move on, Sara. Do not be afraid. You need to find the light and go towards it. Your mother will be there, Sara. She is waiting for you. Go to the light and you will not be frightened anymore, I promise."

Then Charlotte spoke softly to the five of us. "Close your eyes and imagine a door opening very slowly, with a white light shining from behind it."

It felt like a real door was actually in front of me, with clean light shining through. A few minutes later, she rang the bell, and we opened our eyes.

"Sara, go to the light, child. Go to the light and your mother will be there. Find the light, Sara." The candles started to jump and waver crazily and I was suddenly shivering with cold, while at the same time my whole body felt charged with electricity. Then a vivid image came to me of the ghostly figures on the farm pond, moving purposefully towards the morning sun on the horizon... towards the light. I was shaking and felt Beth and Mom tighten their grip on my hands.

Charlotte repeated the instructions while continuing to ring the bell. "Go to the light, Sara," she repeated, then to my surprise beckoned to Sara's mother as well. "Gertrude Hall, help Sara come through to you. Help her come through to the light. Go to the light now, Sara. Don't be afraid. Go to Mommy, Sara. Mommy is waiting for you."

The candles went still, and the electricity and coldness vacated my body with a suddenness and energy that left me reeling. The bell was silent.

"Now, blow out the candles gently and wave the smoke about with your hand," Charlotte told us. We moved forward and each blew out a candle and scattered the smoke.

Charlotte then asked us to hold hands again. "Close your eyes and imagine that door slowly closing," and she counted backwards from ten to one. Then she whispered, "I call on little Sara's ancestors to love and care for her and to keep her safe forevermore."

I was completely, indescribably, exhausted. But I also felt peaceful and calm, and wondered if that tranquility was emanating from little Sara. I believe it was.

Chapter Thirty-Nine

London | September, 2005
Day Ten

On the following day, the London skies graced us with sunshine. Beth was booked on a late evening flight, and the next day Mom and I would start our two-week road trip around England, Scotland, and Wales. Mom had said her goodbyes to Beth the previous night and was holed up at the university, finishing off last minute tasks.

That last day together, Beth and I sampled the Hop-On Hop-Off bus and did some other touristy stuff. We admired the decidedly serious Westminster Abbey, wandered down Birdcage Walk to admire stately Big Ben, then walked across Westminster Bridge to ride the un-stately and not-so-serious ferris-wheel they called the London Eye. We crossed back over the Thames on the Jubilee Bridge, and completed brass rubbings at St. Martin-in-the-Fields. We visited the Tower of London, heard the history, saw the prisons, and stood in line to see the Crown Jewels. At Trafalgar Square we took pictures of ourselves perched on those same stately bronze lions that Great Grandma Sadie had referred to in her diary.

I think my favourite part of the day was actually eating our lunch on the lawns of St. Paul's Cathedral. The beautiful dome stood before a backdrop of vivid blue sky and slowly drifting bright clouds. To mimic Jesse, it was "outstanding."

Later, while twilight settled over the city, Beth and I enjoyed a farewell glass of wine in the hotel lobby bar. Through the window we saw the streetlights blink on, and before long, Beth's taxi pulled up. We gathered her belongings and walked outside.

Once her gear was stowed in the boot, Beth turned to face me and I took both her hands in mine. The doe eyes and cat eyes held gazes. "Beth," I said, but that was as far as I got before my throat clenched and my eyes started to overflow.

Her eyes shone with tears and she squeezed my hands. "I know," was all she said, but it was enough.

Then we threw ourselves at each other in a tight hug,

and I didn't want to let her go. But all too quickly, she was in the cab waving out the back window, and I was left on the sidewalk, gulping and sniffing and smiling all at the same time. Turning around, I spied an old friend sailing full-blown above the trees in Kensington Park.

"Hello Moon," I said, not caring if the doorman heard me. "Did you see that? We did it. I told you we would. We did it." And there I stood, gazing blurredly at Moon, taking big shaky breaths and grinning like a fool.

Later, while lying on the bed in my hotel room, I remembered hearing something on the radio months before. It said your siblings are the people in your life who will know you the longest. As you grow older, they are the only ones who really know where you came from; the only ones who share lifelong memories. Now Beth and I would share those lifetime memories and our future children would make memories together too. We did it.

Chapter Forty

Britain | October, 2005

My mom and I spent just over two weeks travelling together in England, Scotland, and Wales. We puzzled over the mystery of Stonehenge, admired the beautiful limestone of Bath, and hiked the rolling countryside of the Lake District. In the Black Mountains, we stood in hushed silence watching wild ponies graze in a misty meadow. We wandered through castles and churches, sampled Scotch whiskey, and gazed into the inky-black waters of Loch Ness during a moonlight ride on the lake. Much to my disappointment, the fabled Loch Ness Monster did not reveal herself.

To my mother's smug amusement, Jesse and I skyped, texted, or emailed daily throughout our trip, and during these discussions we analyzed all my family mysteries. Since little Sara was buried, I had not been disturbed by either the coffin or the Rasputin nightmare. I had not seen little Sara at all, either in my dreams or when awake. It seemed that both the little girl and her brother Isaac had needed her to be found, acknowledged, and properly buried. Jesse pointed out that my coffin dream was not about a coffin at all. The confinement, blackness, and terror apparently simulated little Sara being wedged into the narrow bottom of the well.

Jesse and I came to the disturbing conclusion that Isaac purposely killed his little sister by pushing her down the well, because there were "too many children," and he thought one less mouth to feed might mean more food for himself. A starving 5-year old killed his 3-year old sister for the chance of a bit more food. But Great-Great Grand-father Isaac—aka Rasputin—was tormented with guilt for the rest of his life. The altered Bible quote pretty much told the story. "What have you done? The voice of your *sister's* blood is crying to Me from the ground. Now you are cursed from the ground, which has opened its mouth to receive your *sister's* blood from your hand." Isaac believed he was cursed and suffered horrible, debilitating guilt for the rest of his life, resulting in a diagnosis of Religious Mania. In today's world, the term schizophrenia would no doubt have been used.

Chapter Forty-One

London to Ontario | October, 2005

During the second week in October, my Mom and I returned to London. The very next day, I boarded an early afternoon flight to Toronto by myself, as Mom had two more months of work at the university. It seemed like a long time since I had left Ontario—or more specifically, since I had left Jesse. He would be picking me up at the airport when I arrived there late in the evening, Ontario time. I could hardly wait.

When I finally navigated through the baggage pick-up at Toronto airport, Jesse greeted me with a mammoth hug and a twirl-around worthy of a movie scene. It was after nine in the evening by that time, and Jesse had arranged for us to stay overnight at a friend's place in Mississauga.

We woke the next morning to a magnificent October day. When Jesse and "Little Miss Sunshine" got us out of the city, I was astonished by the fall kaleidoscope of colours. The exuberant sugar maples flaunted their oranges and reds, providing a striking contrast to the soft golds of the demure birch. In areas further out of the city, dark moody evergreens provided a dramatic backdrop. It was amazing, and I couldn't stop pointing and exclaiming. Jesse laughed and shook his head at every new adjective. He took a route north that was unknown to me, but eventually I saw a sign for Maple Ridges Conservation Authority and he turned onto a gravel road.

"Would it be okay if we went for a little hike?" he asked.

I was thrilled, and for the next two hours we savoured the pure autumn air and the astonishing landscape. The vivid trees and dark rock outcroppings of the escarpment were staged against a vibrant blue sky. It was mesmerizing. At a high look-out point I threw my arms out wide and announced, "I could look at this view forever!"

Jesse echoed with a quiet "Me too," but when glancing his way, I realized he wasn't looking at the view, he was looking straight at me. My hair blew wildly over my face but I pinned it back with one arm, and we stood there grinning at each other, as though we both knew a secret we were just bursting to tell.

"Ginger, have you ever been told you have a killer smile?" he asked.

Taking two steps towards him, I grasped the front of

his shirt with both hands, and looked up into those slate-blue eyes. "Yes, in fact, someone has, and I've also been described as a great kisser."

"Well," he said, "I better check that out." And he did. Then he caught two handfuls of my wild, blowing mane and looked me in the eyes again. "Outstanding," he said and leaned down for another kiss.

After the hike, Jesse drove to Orangeville, where we had lunch in a cute little bistro. Then, back in the car, we headed north again, and he started peppering me with questions about my "Sara Quest." Even though I had told him every detail by email, text, or phone, he wanted to hear the whole story again. Finally, when he seemed satisfied, I asked him about school and his family, and before long we crossed the old bridge at Scone and were back on the County Line. I was excited to see Grandma and Grandpa and my Dad, who I knew had spent the previous week at the farm, helping to "batten down the hatches for Old Man Winter." On that amazing day it seemed like winter was a long way off, but I guessed it could come swirling along at any time.

As we pulled into the lane, I cried out, "Look at all the people!" Jesse just grinned in a knowing manner.

There were little kids puddling at the water's edge with nets, two of my teenage cousins were fishing from the canoe, and some aunts and uncles were in the middle of a bocce ball game on the pond lawn. I tumbled out of the car and raced towards Grandpa, the closest person to me.

"Grandpa!" I shouted. "Everyone is here!"

"Yep, the whole fam-dam-ly," Grandpa said as he gave me a bear hug,

Then Maggie and Brandon charged up and insisted I look at frogs in their buckets. I looked and admired, and laughed and hugged.

It turned out that the last person I got to was Grandma. "There's my girl," she said and hugged me hard and long. When she finally released me, there were tears trickling down the creases in her old cheeks.

"Grandma, what is it?" I asked with alarm.

She took a shaky breath. "I have another surprise for you," she said.

I was facing towards the pond and she grasped my shoulders and turned me around to look in the opposite direction. There was a man just coming out of the garage carrying a cooler, while two of my little nephews tumbled around him like puppies, yapping and giggling. The man looked straight at me and smiled.

For a moment it didn't register, then it hit me like a physical force that took my breath away. It was Uncle Ray! He had never smiled at me before. Ever.

My mouth hung open in amazement as Uncle Ray strode towards me, put the cooler on a nearby picnic table, and stood looking at me with a big grin on his face. I was speechless. "Uncle Ray, I'm speechless," I said.

He took a big breath and said, "Is it okay if I hug you?"

I stepped forward and reached for him and he hugged me hard. Then he held me away from him a bit and said,

"Sara, I have not felt this well for as long as I can remember. I have not had a vision or hallucination since you buried the little girl."

I broke down into full-blown sobbing and he hugged me again. "You are my hero," he whispered into my hair, which made me cry even harder. I'd never been anyone's hero before.

Hours later, snuggled into my third floor bed, I gazed up through the skylight at the stars and smiled. It had been a riotous afternoon and evening of frog hunting, games, campfire, and (as per usual) massive amounts of food. Uncle Ray participated in all the activities with a vitality and eagerness that took my breath away.

Around the campfire, the family insisted that Beth and I recount in full detail, our story of finding little Sara and giving her peace. During the home stretch of the story, while describing the service with the psychic medium at the cemetery, we both became quite choked up and could barely finish. I saw worried expressions exchanged around the fire, and Jesse put his hand on my back.

Then Beth stood up and babbled, "I think we're crying with happiness!"

I nodded, and started wailing full-out, as Beth and I tumbled into each other's arms.

"I'd hate to see them when they're actually upset about something!" Cory quipped, and everyone laughed, including Beth and I through our tears.

Thankfully, at that point, Jesse asked, "How about the four of us take a walk around the pond?"

We nodded wordlessly, so Jesse grabbed a flashlight off the picnic table, and we headed out. By the time we reached the far side of the water, Beth and I were actually presenting like reasonably normal people again. The four of us stopped and gazed across the pond to the campfire and the collection of family, and Jesse gave my hand two quick squeezes. I responded with two squeezes back, took in a big slow breath, and thought how amazing it was to have him by my side, and how lucky I was to be part of such an incredible family.

Later in the evening, while the young kids twirled sparklers in the dusky twilight, my mind drifted back to little Sara. I believed she was comforted by our efforts on her behalf. Hopefully, she had moved past her pain and loneliness, and had found solace in the spirit world somewhere in the beyond. With the party over, and me snuggled into my attic bed, I reached over and touched the face of the doll perched on my beside table.

"Goodbye Sara," I whispered. "Goodbye."

Chapter Forty-Two

It was the last Friday in October. I'd been back from England for almost three weeks and had not had a single nightmare, nor seen little Sara during the day or night. Jess was driving up that afternoon, and taking me to Port Elgin for dinner and then Beth and Corry were arriving later in the evening.

My entire day had been spent picking, peeling, and cooking apples. Perched on a step-ladder that morning, I was mesmerized by the indigo backdrop of autumn sky against the apple redness. It felt like I was suspended in front of a magnificent painting. The local geese were busy making winter plans, and I tracked the progress of a muddled troop of them that argued and squabbled their way across the sky in scraggly procession. Pathetic. Shortly after though, another unit traversed the sky in a perfect V formation, with the leader honking out crisp commands— now that was more like it.

Grandma and I made a huge apple crisp, as well as nine jars of applesauce. Then I shooed her off to an easy chair in the big room and cleaned up the kitchen stickiness, all while savouring the sweet cinnamon smells. When the job was almost done, I glanced out the window towards the pond, then immediately pitched the dish cloth in the sink and took off.

"Grandma, Grandpa, look at the lighting!" I called, as I charged out the door.

Sometimes in the fall, mother nature graces the landscape with a few moments of the most amazing, mesmerizing light. The contrasts are sharper, the shadows are longer, and the whole landscape seems to hold its breath in anticipation... of what, I don't know. There was a subtle eeriness in the air, and I walked around the pond, absorbing it all. A contingency of five geese circled around and landed on the water in unison, and as I paused at the far bank, I saw that Grandma and Grandpa were standing on the deck.

Just as the surreal light started to slide away, my phone rang. I almost ignored it, but at the third ring decided to answer and responded to the caller with a few "yes-es," a "certainly," and finally a "thank you so very much."

After hitting the "end call" button, I threw my hands in the air, let out a whoop, and charged off towards the house, causing the geese to lift off the water in a honking, flapping protest. While clattering over the bridge, through the willow garden, and on towards the deck, I shouted, "Grandma, Grandpa, I have a job! I have a plan! I'm going to be a grown-up after all!"

Taking the deck steps two at a time, I threw my arms around the two of them together and did a standing-in-place, modified happy-dance. They laughed and Grandma slapped at my shoulder to let her go, then put her hands on either side of my face, and looked into my eyes.

"I never doubted you for a moment, dear," she said, then sat down on the seat of her walker and asked for details.

The phone call was an offer to cover for a year-long maternity leave in Walkerton, a town about a half-hour drive from the farm. The assignment was to teach a grade two class, starting at the beginning of December.

Grandpa put his arm around my shoulder and said, "So you're going to be a country girl… glad to hear it!"

"I'm really happy about that too, Grandpa…I like this country life! But Jesse will be here soon, so I'd better get ready for dinner. My plan is to wait and give him my news at the restaurant, then we can have a toast and a celebration dinner."

With a twinkle in her eye, Grandma nodded, smiled a sneaky smile, and said "uh-huh."

An hour later, the three of us were sitting at the table in the big room, when Jesse drove in and parked. Grandma peeked at me out of the corner of her eye, while Grandpa looked straight out the window with a grin on his face.

I twitched. I fidgeted. I stretched out my arms and clasped my hands together on top of the table. Then jumping up and charging towards the door, I called back, "You're right, you're right, I can't wait to tell him!"

Jesse let out a whoop with my news and lifted me up in a big bear hug. Then we waved at Grandma and Grandpa, climbed into "Little Miss Sunshine," and headed to Port Elgin. Although it was pretty chilly, being as how we were tough Canadians, we decided to sit on the patio for a drink before we went inside for dinner at the beachside restaurant. After further discussing every aspect of my teaching offer, Jesse informed me that he had some news too. One of his professors learned Jesse wanted to work at the power plant near Port Elgin, and apparently had a friend in the Human Resources department, and would contact her with a good recommendation. It would be so perfect if Jess was able to get a job in the area too!

It was my turn to toast him, and then we gazed towards the lake and the disappearing sun. A bright band of gold sat on the horizon while thick clouds crowded the sky above, blocking out the sun altogether. But as we watched, the sun moved into that open strip, and by some trick of light refraction, suddenly presented as two fiery orange suns stacked one on top of the other. It was a stunning surreal image that lasted only a moment, then quickly merged into one sun and dropped below the horizon.

By nine o'clock, we were back at the farm with a campfire blazing and tiki lamps gleaming around the circumference of the pond, like beacons in the night for Beth and Cory. The flames cast wavering, elongated reflections on the water, and made me think of hidden castles and watery mysteries below the surface. A sliver of moon hung suspended in the sky and the Big Dipper dangled above us, pouring invisible water into the pond.

Before long, we heard the beep of a car horn, signalling that Beth and Cory had arrived. They went into the house briefly and then joined us at the campfire, and we spent the next couple hours catching up. They were both very pleased about our job-related news, and then we caught up on their life in the city. Eventually Beth asked about Uncle Ray.

"Oh, he's doing so great," I said. "He's been spending five mornings a week helping at the animal shelter in Owen Sound, and is talking with Grandpa and Grandma about the possibility of opening a doggy daycare."

"That would be amazing!"

"Yes, if he keeps making such great progress, Grandpa and Grandma would provide the start-up money. He's put on some weight, talks a lot more, and seems really good. Grandpa says Ray's counsellor thinks he can move out of the group home soon."

"Wow," said Beth. "That is so great." She added more wood to the fire. "Hey, do you two have any plans for New Year's Eve?"

"New Years!" I said. "That seems so long away, but I guess it really isn't."

"Well, we have friends with an apartment in downtown Ottawa," Cory said, "and they're going away for two weeks over Christmas and New Year's, and offered us their place for a few days if we want. So we were wondering if you'd like to join us to celebrate New Year's in Ottawa."

"It would be fun," Beth added in, "We could spend probably fours days there... go skating on the Rideau Canal and cross country skiing in Gatineau Park. And on New Year's Eve there's a big outdoor party and concert on Sparks Street, plus fireworks at the Parliament Buildings."

Jesse and I agreed that it sounded great, then Jesse stood and held out his beer. "I would like to make a toast, so you need to quiet down and listen carefully." We did as we were told, and waited for him to grace us with some pearl of wisdom. "Happy New Year!" he bellowed, and we all laughed and clinked our bottles together. In the dark, I could not stop grinning to myself—more memory-making coming up!

Shortly afterwards, I promised a treat and headed to the house, throwing Moon a grin and a quick thumbs-up en route. After heating up four big bowls of apple crisp and finding a tray to put them on, I headed back to the camp-fire. We all savoured the sweet autumn treat while the evening air chilled around us. Everyone became quiet and soon we decided to call it a night. Beth volunteered to snuff out the tiki lamps, so she and Cory headed off in the dark around the pond.

I drew my chair a little closer to the fire, but Jesse took my hand, pulled me onto his lap, and wrapped his arms around me. We couldn't see Beth and Cory in the dark, but the first tiki flame blinked out, then after a couple minutes the next one disappeared as well. We silently witnessed the rhythm of the vanishing flares around the pond, which seemed like a count-down to the end of summer.

Putting my arms over Jesse's arms I hugged myself into him. When the final tiki expired, my eyes turned down to the dancing, swirling campfire.

"Outstanding," I said, then turned my head and kissed him on the cheek.

Author's Note

Seeking Sara is a work of fiction, but the inspiration for the book arose from the real-life histories and personalities of my parents and my paternal grandmother. Sara's grandparents in the novel are accurate depictions of my own parents in their later years. The farm that is central to the story, is actually where I lived growing up. My husband and I have owned the farm for many years, and returned to live here full-time a few years ago.

The wartime stories in *Seeking Sara* are re-tells of my parents experiences (including my father being 24 hours late for his own wedding). The early farm stories are also true events, including the winter conditions when they moved in, the previous owners who would not leave, and the mysterious man who was confined to an upstairs room.

My grandmother did lose her hearing due to working in a boot factory in London from the age of 15 to 25. In 1920, she immigrated by herself to Canada… disembarking in Montreal. My portrayal of her life in Canada is generally accurate, although unfortunately, she did not to my knowledge, keep any diaries. When I was a teenager and young adult, my grandmother lived in a mobile home on our farm.

Sometime prior to my grandmother immigrating to Canada, her father (my great-grandfather) was committed to the *City of London Lunatic Asylum/Stone Sanatorium.* He later died within that institution of a mental disorder that was labelled as "Religious Mania."

A few years ago my husband and I holidayed in London and managed to find the home that my grandmother lived in, and also the church she attended prior to moving to Canada. As described in the novel, St. Ann's Church was beautiful both inside and out, with the the rose window being a highlight. The current owners of her house were unfortunately away, but a neighbour spoke to us, and pointed out that a scattering of houses up and down the street were of a different architecture than most homes. This was because several of the houses had been hit by bombs during the war and eventually rebuilt in a very dissimilar style.

In our office at the farm, in the original large oval frame, is a beautiful photo of my parents, shortly after their wedding, with my father in his air force uniform. As well, we have a framed display containing my Grandmother's small boot hammer, her *Membership Certificate for The London Metropolitan Branch of the National Union of Boot and Shoe Operatives*, as well as her *Letter of Recommendation from* Flatau & Co, Shoe Manufacturers, dated August 17, 1920.

My parents and my grandmother were strong, determined, courageous people. They lived through World Wars and the Great Depression. They confronted personal hardships and challenges in their lives, that would have defeated many of us. It is a privilege for me to share a small part of their story with others.

About the Author

Maurine Gillberry (nee Pitt), grew up on a farm near Chesley, Ontario. After finishing high school and a teaching degree, she taught elementary school in her home area for three years, and then moved to Calgary, Alberta to complete a Masters in Educational Psychology. Returning to Ontario, Maurine worked for many years as a Psychology Associate in a large Toronto-area school board.

Maurine and her husband have now retired to the farm she grew up on. Maurine enjoys many outdoor activities, as well as travelling, reading, and spending time with her two daughters and their young families.

A huge special thank you to my good friend, Connie Sweiger. Without your significant editing efforts and encouragement, *Seeking Sara* would never have become a reality.